Books by M K Scott

Cupid's Catering Company
Culinary Cozy Mystery
Wedding Cake Blues
Truffle Me Not
Double Chocolate Deception

The Talking Dog Detective Agency
Cozy Mystery

✧   ✧   ✧

A Bark in the Night
Requiem for a Rescue Dog Queen
Bark Twice for Danger
The Ghostly Howl
Dog Park Romeo
On St. Nick's Trail

The Painted Lady Inn Mysteries Series
Culinary Cozy Mystery

✧   ✧   ✧

Murder Mansion
Drop Dead Handsome
Killer Review

Christmas Calamity

Death Pledges a Sorority

Caribbean Catastrophe

Weddings Can be Murder

The Skeleton Wore Diamonds

Death of a Honeymoon

Cakewalk to Murder

Sailors Take Warning

Two Many Sleuths

The Way Over the Hill Gang Series
Cozy Mystery

✦   ✦   ✦

Late for Dinner

Late for Bingo

Late for Shuffleboard

Late for Square Dancing

Late for Love

Late for the Wedding

The Tenacious Librarian Series
Culinary Cozy Mystery

Bullies, Bovines, and a Bookmobile

Frogs, Floods, and Fraud (June 2023)

Bullies, Bovines and a Bookmobile

The Tenacious Librarian Series

M K Scott

Bullies, Bovines and a Bookmobile

M K Scott

Copyright © 2022

Print Edition

Chapter One

THE LATE AFTERNOON sun bathed the aging craftsman-style home in a warm glow. The house featured a wide porch with a green glider and blue Adirondack chairs. Tenny, a thirty-ish redhead with an Irish cream complexion along with a tendency to freckle, tugged on the waist of her ill-fitting black suit while attempting to keep her balance in her classic black pumps. The suit, never a favorite of hers, made an appearance only on important occasions, such as job interviews. The wool blend fabric, heavy on the wool part, chafed her delicate skin despite the practical cotton blouse and slip that should have shielded her. Fortunately, she'd donned it for only one interview, snagged the job, and then put it away until today.

The house served as a beacon, sending out its message of sanctuary—something Tenny coveted considering the horrible morning and a good part of the afternoon she'd just endured. Her hand covered her heart as she drew closer to the bright red geraniums, purple and white petunias cascading over the sides of their terracotta pots, and perky, golden marigolds. The velvety petals and thick green leaves were due to her aunt Bernadette's green thumb. Some of her aunt's friends called her Bernie or Bert, but most used her nickname, Cinnamon, after her grand champion cinnamon buns. No one had managed to steal her title, though many had tried.

Tenny wiped away a tear and swallowed hard. There'd be a new champion this year.

Earlier, at the funeral, all her aunt's friends either patted her shoulder or engulfed her in unexpected perfumed hugs. Many were so distraught they hung onto Tenny for reassurance as opposed to the other way around. A few took the opportunity to ask about Willow, her aunt's sister, and technically Tenny's biological mother. Her back molars slammed together, both irritated that they had asked and the fact that her absentee mother had given them the opportunity to do so. "I suspect she'd have come if she'd known, but we have no forwarding address."

That morsel resulted in the busybodies clicking their tongues in disapproval and hurrying away to spread the news. That's life in a small town. Everyone knew your business and what they didn't know they wouldn't hesitate to ask—or at least that applied to Gloria Swenson, more commonly referred to as Buzzy. Her nickname was well-earned since she flew from person to person, both gathering and depositing gossip rather like an ambitious, nosy bee.

Comments about her mother, she brushed aside. She had heard it all before. Besides, her aunt served as her actual mother. For the most part, Tenny tried not to think about Willow. She refused to call her mother. It didn't matter, since Willow never showed up to notice Tenny's small acts of rebellion. Anger replaced sadness and about the time she'd worked up a good mad, chewing on the subject, someone called her name.

A petite, plump, blonde woman in a pink floral dress hurried her way, waving as she picked her way over the aging sidewalk. It had buckled in some sections as if intentionally planning to trip the unwary. Tenny bit her bottom lip, hoping her old friend Blue wouldn't fall prey to rough pavement. As a dairy farmer, a pair of rubber farm boots served as Blue's everyday footwear as opposed to heels. Dressed in her Sunday best, Blue had to be even more out of her comfort zone than Tenny.

"No rush!" Tenny called out. "I'll still be here when you get here."

A few minutes later, Blue pulled to a stop with a gasp in front of Tenny. She lifted one foot, pulled off her shoe with a vengeance, and repeated the action until she was standing in her stocking feet. "I hate these stupid shoes."

"You'll ruin your hose," Tenny cautioned and gestured toward the porch as their destination.

An exasperated sigh came from Blue. "I hope I do. Pantyhose are the creation of the devil or, at the very least, a man who never, ever had to wear them. Anytime I pull on a pair, I ruin them. Couldn't expect these to last. There's already a run in them. See?" She lifted the dress hem a little to expose a long run, starting at her thigh and shooting upward.

"How did you manage that?" Tenny asked as she strolled toward her house. She placed her foot on the porch step and turned, waiting for her friend.

Blue shrugged. "I don't know. You know me and fancy clothes. We don't go together. I'd say we're allergic to each other. Maybe the hose tried to get away."

Her friend's description made her chuckle on a day she would have sworn nothing would make her laugh. "I know what you mean. This suit is driving me crazy. Come inside and you can shed your hose. Won't your husband need you back at the farm soon?"

"Oh, no." Blue gave a vigorous shake of her head. "Griffin's

3

training the assistants for when we need to travel. You know he likes things a certain way, and so do our girls."

Anyone else might think the term girls referred to children as opposed to their dairy cows, who Blue named after mythical characters. At one time, she named them after goddesses, but it became confusing with multiple Venuses, Heras, and Athenas.

Tenny pushed the front door open and stepped into the quiet living room. For a second or two, she forgot to answer, listening to the silence—if you could call it *listening*. Maybe she absorbed the silence or accepted it more as a preview of her future life without her aunt or her uncle, who'd died earlier that year. Could she deal with this?

Many at the funeral suggested her aunt died from heartsickness and followed her husband. The thought annoyed Tenny, since it implied that her aunt had abandoned *her* as opposed to dying from cancer.

A throat clearing along with the slight click of the front door shutting signaled Blue's entry into the house. Tenny shook her head, trying to return to the conversation topic. "You want someone the girls can get along with? Are you planning a trip?"

Even though Tenny prompted the question, she wanted to withdraw it. She'd lived in the tiny town of Emerson most of her life, and she knew everyone, but there were very few she'd call friends. Blue happened to be the only one she'd trust with her secret dreams. Well, besides her aunt Cinnamon. Now, it was just Blue and it looked like she might be taking off.

"Not really." Blue wrinkled her pert nose and shimmied out of her hose, throwing them up in the air with a flourish. They both chuckled at her action, but a flushed Blue picked up her hose and deposited them into the wicker waste basket kept near the telephone stand. Time moved more slowly in Emerson, Indiana, and people still used landlines—not too surprising since cell towers were few and far between, which meant dropped calls.

"You need to get your help ready before you need them." Blue wrinkled her nose and added, "Wish we didn't have to train extra help—and Cody could handle everything." Blue plopped down onto the divan with a sigh.

"Cody?" Tenny's brow wrinkled as she tried to put a face to the name. "Should I know a Cody?"

"Not really. He's new to Emerson. Got fired from Darling Dairy and Griffin felt sorry for him and hired him about a year ago. We try to keep the dairy small enough that just the two of us can handle it, but sometimes it takes more than us. He works only a couple of days a week. Sometimes, he's okay." She worked her chin one way, then the other, pressed her lips together, and then spoke. "Other days…" She left the sentence unfinished. Talking trash about people didn't bother most folks, but Blue tried to abstain—with the exception of Rita, the town's unofficial queen and resident mean girl.

"What about that couple you used the last time you guys took off?" Tenny called over one shoulder as she made her way to the kitchen. Courtesy demanded she procure a cold drink for her guest, especially on a hot day like today. Foil-wrapped pie pans and aluminum tin pans with plastic covers revealed cakes, cookies, and brownies. The community really had come together when it came to the funeral food train. What could stay out on the counter did. Other food offerings she crammed into the fridge or the outside freezer. "Can I get you a piece of pie? Cake? Maybe a brownie?"

"Oh…" Blue drew out the word and somehow packed it with

both reluctance and longing. While most people loved a chubby baby, somehow the love lessened as the child aged and remained plump, which might explain the why behind all the various diets. Close scrutiny of the wide-hipped women on her mother's side revealed the futility of chasing the thigh gap that current fashion promoted.

Tenny stuck her head out of the kitchen. "You know you do. If not, could you at least take one of the cakes or pies home to your hubby? I'll have to put it into a different pan…" She crinkled her nose. "…because."

"Yeah, I know," Blue agreed. "Got to get those pans back to the right person. A brownie. Just one." She held up one finger for emphasis.

With sweating glasses of iced tea and a small, faded floral dish with two brownies on it weighing down the tray, Tenny returned to the living room. "What about the couple you used last year?" Tenny prompted, proud she could remember the original topic.

Blue paused and sniffed dismissively. "They now work with…" She hesitated. "Beef cattle. A lot less work."

"I can't imagine beef cattle need *any* work."

"They don't. Occasionally, they get on the wrong side of the fence, usually after pushing it down. Of course, Angus tend to be more adventurous." Blue accepted the glass of tea, arranging one foot underneath her as Tenny peeled off her jacket and took her seat. "I didn't come here to talk about my cows. What about you? What are your plans?"

It was the same question she had asked herself the last three days. Taking an audible breath, she waited as if the answer would suddenly form. It didn't. "Aunt Cinnamon loved the library, loved reading. No one was prouder when I received my library sciences degree. Told everyone about my job at the university. Even when I ran Emerson's small library for the few months it existed, she'd strut around the town more pleased than a chicken with one egg. I never let her know the town voted down the ten-dollar per family annual tax increase to support the library. Right before she died, she kept talking about reaching out to other areas without libraries. How it wasn't right some folks had nothing decent to read. Not sure what she expected me to do, especially since I couldn't even keep our own library open."

Blue put down her tea glass on the water-ringed pie crust table and reached for her friend's hand. "You did all you could do. I know plenty of folks who wanted a library, but you got the ignorant who refused the annual library tax, which amounted to the cost of three energy drinks—two if you buy them in town. What about the town council? You said you were going to petition them."

"I did…" Tenny admitted, glancing over to where a stack of unopened mail waited. "They sent me a written reply, which can't be good."

"Maybe," Blue offered. "Maybe not. You'll never know until you open it."

"You're right." A heavy sigh escaped her. "I'll do that tomorrow."

Chapter Two

THE HALF-OPEN FLOWER-EDGED curtains revealed the shuttered blinds that kept out most of the late afternoon sun, creating a shadowy, relaxed interior for the conversing women. Bees buzzed around the porch blooms, adding to the sleepy atmosphere produced by the hot, sticky summer day where any movement felt like a monumental effort.

Blue gestured to the stack of mail resting precariously on a side table. "You really need to go through it. What if there are bills to be paid? You could get your electricity turned off. You don't want it turned off in this heat wave we're having."

Instead of replying, Tenny picked up her sweating glass of iced tea and took a sip. Her friend made sense, which she usually did—another reason she rated high on the friendship scale. Tenny had put everything on hold when her aunt revealed her cancer diagnosis. Even though her aunt insisted she didn't want Tenny leaving her university job, Tenny made her explanations at work and headed home. There was no way the woman who raised her would end her days in a hospital. Funny thing was, what she assumed would be weeks stretched into months. In the intervening time, she helped set up a small store front library for the town, fulfilling her aunt's dream.

At first, Cinnamon acted pretty much the same, although she tired easily, ate little, and would sometimes fall asleep in mid-conversation. Those last few weeks they spent doing ordinary things, such as talking, cooking, and gardening. The last two chores Tenny did while her aunt Cinnamon supervised. Even though Tenny knew how to deal with a root-bound plant, she stayed quiet as her aunt explained in detail. Her uncle Mark said people say what they do for their own purposes, not for yours, which meant a joke heard a dozen times should be endured with a smile.

All the same, maybe she should take a peek at the mail while Blue was here. Without speaking, she rose from her seat and drifted over to the table, picking up the pile before plopping back down beside her friend. She gave half the mail to Blue. "You nagged me. Now you have to help. A good part of it is junk mail. Let's filter out any bills or sympathy cards. The last I'll have to remember to thank the senders when I see them, if only on Cinnamon's behalf. She considered good manners almost as important as reading."

"Good thing she couldn't witness how some of her so-called friends acted at the funeral," Blue sniffed, tossing a couple of craft store ads to the floor.

A long sigh escaped as Tenny reached up and rubbed the back of her neck. "They weren't that bad. Then again, I might just be in a stupor since everything happened so fast. The questions about Willow I expected." She rubbed one arm, then the other, before picking up some mail. "What I didn't expect," she turned to face Blue and crinkled her nose, "were all those mamas offering up their single sons, so I wouldn't be all alone in this big house."

Blue hooted, snickering so hard that she dropped the mail in her hands. The hearty response coaxed a smile from Tenny. "I'm glad you can see the humor in it. After I got over my initial shock, I think I mumbled something about being okay. I may have mentioned something about getting a dog."

"Ha! A dog?" Blue slapped the couch. "I can imagine which mamas offered up the sons they haven't been able to get out of their house with a crowbar, and you say, 'No thanks. A dog will suit me just fine.'"

"I didn't say exactly that." She rolled her eyes upward. "Who knows what I said and who I offended?"

"Don't worry about it." Blue smirked. "Plenty of the local girls chose not to take up their failure-to-launch sons." She held up one finger. "I did notice Dallas spending a great deal of time beside you. His ex, Rita, noticed, too. She scowled during the whole funeral, which made me giggle."

"Oh." Tenny tilted her head and sent a mock stern look at her friend. "You were the giggler? Good to know. As for Dallas," her shoulders went up in a shrug, "he's just a nice guy. It's who he is ever since his family moved into town when we all started sixth grade. All the girls went crazy over a boy they hadn't known all their lives."

"It didn't hurt that he had all that gorgeous blond hair and blue eyes," Blue teased. "He was a cutie back then, but now…" She wolf-whistled.

"Stop it! He's a nice guy, that's all."

"What did the *nice guy* say all that time he spent by your side?"

Her brow furrowed as she tried to recall. "Didn't talk a great deal—he was more of a presence. He did say if I needed any help to call."

Blue clapped her hands together. "Bingo! Told ya."

"That means nothing."

"Sez you. Time will tell." She pursed her lips and tapped her temple. "If I remember correctly, he ended up in your group whenever we did group work in class."

"Please." Tenny gave a short, dismissive snort. "Everyone wanted to be in my group because I knew how to research, outline, and pull things together. I practically did everything. Getting the others to work made me feel like a draft horse at the state fair, pulling the heavy skid on my own."

"Are you telling me Dallas didn't pull his own weight?"

Even though over two decades had passed since sixth grade, she could remember it like yesterday. "No," she acknowledged with a head shake. "He worked. And on occasion, came up with better ideas than I did."

Tenny nudged her friend with an elbow. "I see what you did there. Got me thinking about something else—even if it was a bit nonsensical. No way Dallas would be interested in me. I suspect those men whose mamas were so quick to offer up would give me a pass, too."

"Don't belittle yourself."

"I'm just stating facts. Before I left town, there was plenty of time to ask me out." She pressed the tips of a thumb and forefinger together, creating a zero. "That's how many dates I had. The same number I've had since I returned to town. It makes me wonder why suddenly I'm so attractive as a potential daughter-in-law."

Blue held up her index finger. "You have an in-town house on the best street. It carries a certain prestige with it. When the grandkids come, there won't be any other grandparents to share them with." She popped up a second finger. "Then there's a big fat inheritance you're supposed to get. Heard it might be millions."

"You heard wrong." Tenny gave a firm nod. "I guess any money is good. My aunt's medical bills will gobble up a fair portion, but there may be a tidy sum left."

"And?" Blue prompted.

"And what?" Tenny inquired, glancing down at a slim envelope in her hand and biting her lip.

"What do you plan to do with the money?"

"Something that would please my aunt. I hoped to buy more books for our little library. Most of the really good readers are already on their second reading of the books we do have." She waved the letter in her hand. "I can only hope the council sees fit to honor my aunt's memory."

With that pronouncement, she slit the envelope open and shook out a folded page. Her eyes went back and forth, scanning the page as the corners of her lips settled into a definite frown. When she finished the letter, she wadded it up and threw it on the floor with the other garbage.

Blue asked, "That bad, huh?"

"Bad enough and pretty much what I expected. How can I honor my aunt with all these roadblocks? There's nothing she loved better than opening up a new mystery novel and trying to solve it before the detective did. You know those little papers I put inside the mystery books?" She waited for her friend's confirmation before continuing. "I put those in for my aunt and people like her who read so many books they can't always remember what they've read. They put their initials on the paper. It's an easy way to see if they've read a book. What am I supposed to do now? They want me to remove all the books by Wednesday. An insurance company will be taking the space over."

"Where will the books go?"

"Wait." Tenny reached for the crumpled paper and smoothed it out. "Oh." She glanced up at her friend. "Let me read it. *For your service on behalf of the community, you may retain any books or shelving you wish.*"

"That's cool. They're giving you your own little library."

A derisive snort escaped her. Rather than say what she initially thought, she took a deep breath and exhaled. "I guess they are. Cinnamon donated the majority of her own personal library. All the same, my aunt had a vision for books to be available to surrounding townships without libraries. I guess our town *now* fits that description, but I'm not sure how I can make it happen. Am I supposed to drive around with boxes of books tucked into my tiny compact car, and then ring a hand bell once I arrive in town?"

Blue pressed her fingertips together. "I like the image. You'll need a schedule to let people know when you'll be in town. You can set it up in a local grocery parking lot or at least near one. That way, you can get some shoppers and their children. Let me grab some paper and a pen, and we can work the details out."

Blue's husband, Griffin, joked that if something needed doing, he just pushed Blue in the general direction and it got done. Sometimes, though, Blue could be a bit overwhelming. "I was joking about books in my car. Even the small number of books we have at the library wouldn't fit into the trunk. It would be more like a yard sale than a library, with people having to lean over and paw through titles in a cardboard box."

"You're right. You need a bus, and it'll need a name. Decide what color you want to paint it. And I have the perfect person to help you with your shelves: Mr. *Call-Me-If-You-Need-Anything*

Dallas."

"I bet he wasn't thinking about shelves when he said that. Besides, I don't know how to drive a bus." As outrageous as the idea was, it had merit—something her aunt would cheer on. Then again, maybe she could just sell the house and hopefully snag another reference librarian job.

"It's no harder than a tractor or a plane," Blue volunteered with a twinkle in her eye.

"I can't operate either of those things."

"No problem." Blue grinned and arched her brows. "Most of the newer models made in 2000 and later are automatic."

"Good to know." Caught up in her friend's enthusiasm, she chuckled. "All we need is a bus."

"Oh, that's easy," Blue exclaimed with a twinkle. "I know a woman with one to sell."

Chapter Three

A N OVERSIZED WOODPECKER continued its early morning hammering on the massive oak that shaded the house. Tenny pulled a needlepointed floral pillow over her head and groaned. The problem with morning is it insisted on starting so early. Birds fell into the program, often breaking into a noisy chorus before dawn. The hammering intensified and almost sounded like glass rattling— that had to be a pileated woodpecker, at least. She pushed the pillow aside and noticed her sun-illuminated room. Tenny blinked twice and reached for her alarm clock, pulling it closer. Without her glasses, the red numerals danced around a bit but settled enough for her to pick out the nine.

"Oh!" She popped up as fast as the spring loader on a stapler and trembled, rather like the spring, realizing she'd forgotten to set her alarm. The hammering morphed into a woman calling her name. "Tenny! I know you're in there. Answer the door!"

Her bare feet hit the floor as she rushed into the living room, not even thinking about her nightshirt emblazoned with bold red and navy words that read: *You had me at pajamas and books.* What could cause someone to show up and pound on her front door? Her anxiety climbed as she darted down the hall, pushing her hair back from her face. The house could be on fire. She sniffed as she passed the kitchen—nothing but a rich cloud of sugar lingering over the baked goods guaranteed to add weight simply by inhaling. Her feet slid a little as she stopped at the door.

Through the door glass panels, she recognized the rounded figure of her aunt's best buddy, Connie Meriweather. As a toddler, she often thought Connie bore a strong resemblance to Cinderella's fairy godmother. Disappointment arrived when she realized the two weren't the same. The kind woman became an unofficial, beloved relative. Her fingers fumbled as she unlocked the door and threw it open. "What's wrong?"

Known for her cheerful, but slow manner of talking, Connie cleared her throat and waited a second before speaking. "I was worried about you, especially when you didn't show up to break down the library. Rita, who I *know* you know, is strutting around, yelling about throwing out everything. I sent the guys she got to help move in her insurance office stuff to the diner for breakfast on my dime. I rushed here to check on you."

Just hearing Rita's name tightened up her shoulders. At college, she used to regale the other students with Rita's diva antics. Her roommate even accused her of making up the story about Rita insisting prom colors had to be changed because they didn't flatter her. People rushed to do Rita's bidding. While a hopeful male might desire to get in good with the cool, superior blonde, most everyone else deferred to avoid a full-blown tantrum. Talk about hateful— they could have saved some letters on the *Mean Girls* movie title and just called it *Rita*. Normally, Tenny avoided the woman, which worked out well since they seldom visited the same places.

Her back molars clamped together as she turned over the possibility that maybe the town wasn't totally against the idea of a library, but more likely Rita's father, who chaired the town council, pushed for the storefront library's closing to score office space for his little darling. After all, he'd already bankrolled several failed businesses, including the *Fairy Tale Princess Dance Studio*. It turned out that girls she mistreated in high school chose not to pay for their daughters to experience the same.

"Sweetie?" Connie prompted in a soft voice. "You really need to come down and load up the books if you want them. I'll be glad to help and can get my husband to bring some boxes from the food store. But we need to hurry. Rita could be dumping the entire children's section into the dumpster as we speak."

"Argh! She wasn't supposed to take possession of the office until tomorrow." Tenny groaned, shot both hands through her hair, and stepped out onto the porch. "It figures! What Rita wants, Rita gets."

"Tenny?"

Of course, Tenny suspected the sweet woman would come up with a pithy saying about keeping her words gentle. She'd probably shocked her aunt's friend with her snarky attitude. Every now and then, things best left unsaid ended up said. "Ah, I know. I sounded bitter."

"Maybe." Connie bobbed her head and wrinkled her nose. "You, along with most of the gals your age, have more than enough reason to resent the unofficial town queen. Not surprising—her mother was the same way, too." She pointed to Tenny's nightshirt. "I like it. I was even with Cinnamon when she bought it. All the same, you'd better go change. We don't want to give the queen any more fodder than she already has."

"Oh, right." Tenny, flushed at the possibility of marching down Main Street in her nightshirt, rushed inside and pulled on a pair of capris and a T-shirt emblazoned with *It's Not Hoarding if it's Books.* She stepped into a pair of canvas deck shoes and scraped her hair into a messy bun. It was not the best look, but there were books on the line. She finished the look by pushing on her glasses, which brought the world into sharper focus. As she walked past the kitchen, she wished for tea, but kept going.

"All right," she announced as she stepped outside for the second time this morning. "Let's go save those books!"

"Yes," Connie agreed, and the two of them turned and headed to the small area they called *downtown*. A feed store, one restaurant with an attached gas station, a hardware store that Uncle Mark used to run, a used car lot, the Food Store, and an oddity store, which sounded better than *junk* shop, served as the sum of their business district.

Her long strides ate up the distance, causing the shorter, less fit Connie to gasp, trying to match the pace. The summer sun spotlighted the buckled sidewalk and summer parched grass. Not even the buildings were spared the scrutiny of the sun that revealed missing shingles or the desperate need for repainting. A freshly polished silver Mercedes convertible parked in front of the library shimmered. Rita's car. Of course, it had to be, since no one else would even think of such an impractical car for use on the dusty country roads.

The sight of it pulled a groan from Tenny. Even though Connie rushed to her house because of Rita's threats to trash the books, it meant her nemesis would obviously be present. The anger that fueled her march toward the little library vanished, leaving an uncertain Tenny staring at the glass display window minus the book village display she'd created. Instead, an ornate sign with extra embellishments that would look more at home in a Victorian parlor rested there. If Tenny squinted, she could just make out the word *insurance*.

Connie nudged her. "Let's get on with it. It's only going to get hotter."

"Yeah, you're right." While not psyched about meeting Rita, she'd do what she usually did all through school—ignore her the best she could. She inhaled and pushed her shoulders back, marched up to the door, and noticed the perfectly pulled-together Rita in a mint linen dress with a waterfall of blonde hair dipping over one eye rather like Veronica Lake, a film star of yesteryear. The henchwoman of choice, Patti Linton, who earned the nickname *Shadow* for how she stuck next to Rita, was doing her bidding. Shadow pushed a scarlet leather loveseat to wherever Rita pointed. Uncertain if she should knock to enter her own library, Tenny set her jaw and swung the door open.

Both women turned toward the door—Shadow, probably glad of the break from moving the same piece of furniture, and Rita, who grumbled, "Oh, there you are!" She gave Tenny a slow perusal, starting at the top of her head all the way down to her toes. "Oh my. You look awful. Tied one on last night?"

A flash of irritation colored her cheeks, but she tamped it down before replying. Uncle Mark used to say the person who reacts in anger loses. No reason to let the vindictive princess know how much she irked her. "No. I may have slept later than usual. Trauma does that to a person. As I recall, you aren't supposed to be here until tomorrow when all the books would have been gone and the place ready for your move-in."

She shrugged her shoulders and gave a slow smile. "Surprise! I'm here now." She waved her hand languidly to where the shelves and table stood haphazardly stacked with books. A couple dozen tomes littered the floor, many open-faced, bending pages and breaking spines.

Book terrorist. She probably never ever bothered to read. Rumor around the school was she had two malleable honor students write out essays on any required reading. Tenny stalked past Rita and scooped up the mistreated books and smoothed their ruffled pages.

The slap of Connie's sensible rubber-soled slip-ons sounded loud on the hardwood floor. Despite the furniture knocked askew in the large room, it sounded empty, as if the soul of the little library had left, leaving only a handful of books and memories. Perhaps needing to fill in the heavy silence that stretched amongst the four of them, Connie chattered. "My hubby will be on his way with the boxes. Later on, once we get them filled, you can tell us where to take them."

Take them. The woman made it sound like she had picked a specific spot to hold the dreams the books represented. Instead of answering, Tenny kneeled and picked up a copy of *Tom Sawyer* from the floor. She closed the open book and noticed the gap caused from lying open—nothing rubber-banding it closed for a bit wouldn't cure. Her gaze lingered on the author's name, Mark Twain. The locals, prone to saddling people with nicknames, and usually not the flattering kind, had named her uncle Mark Twain years ago for his storytelling. Originally, the moniker meant liar, but her uncle took it and ran with it. Most younger folks, her friends included, assumed Mark was his given name since it lacked the peculiarity of other nicknames, such as *Termite* or *Husker*. Somehow, her uncle's nickname story faded since it happened over a half-century ago.

BULLIES, BOVINES AND A BOOKMOBILE

Whoever thought to shame her uncle lost that day.

"For now," she turned to address Connie, "I guess we'll drop the books off at Aunt Cinnamon's house."

"Your house," Connie pointed out with a lifted brow.

"I guess you're right." She managed a small nod. It was too great a change. She'd rather not consider it. The cozy home filled with delicious smells and happy memories often served as her sanctuary, her safe place, but now, not so much, since it lacked the joyous business of Aunt Cinnamon and the laid-back wisdom of Uncle Mark. She gave the book another glance and placed it on the table. "We might as well get started."

Rita deliberately raised her voice. "It's past time you get started." She stood and pressed a hand to her back. "Patti and I are heading out to the new coffee shop at the edge of town for some liquid refreshment since we've been working hard all morning. You girls need to be done by the time I get back."

A giggle erupted from one of the two women as they left. Connie grunted as the door shut. "As a church-going woman, I can't say what I really think. However, I do think it's time for that particular female to move on. We all kind of hoped when the divorce came through that somehow, she'd be ashamed and move somewhere else."

"You'd think," Tenny agreed as she balanced a stack of rescued books on the table. "I'm sure she spun it to her advantage." Tenny knelt to gather up more books. "Not sure what Dallas saw in her besides the obvious beautiful exterior."

"That's a mystery for sure," Connie replied as she straightened a small pile of children's books. "Rita claims Dallas was abusive, and *she* wanted the divorce. Ha!"

As a boy, he had rescued bees and spiders from the classroom before they were swatted. Therefore, the abuse claim felt patently false. "I guess it depends on how she defines *abuse*. He probably told her no when she wanted to do something extravagant."

"Could be," Connie agreed, leaning closer. "I have it on good authority that Dallas started the divorce proceedings. There's a mystery you might want to solve."

Chapter Four

THE LATE MORNING sun seared the east-facing library windows. Tenny wiped away sweat droplets dotting her forehead with the back of her hand. She straightened from her kneeling position next to a produce box filled with dog-eared paperbacks. A couple of feet away, a red-faced Connie closed a filled box. Catching Tenny's attention, she managed a weak smile. What a gem! There was no reason for her to spend her day packing up books, but she did without a complaint.

Tenny walked over to the windows to pull down the shades the way she did every morning she had spent there. It allowed the patrons to read in a much softer light and alleviated some of the heat. Only, when she reached for the shades, there was nothing there. Turning her head upward, she noticed the empty space where the shades had been. "Where are my shades?"

The bell on the door jangled as Connie moved closer and joined in the upward stare. "What shades?"

A skipped breakfast and no lunch resulted in hunger and contributed to her growing irritability—along with the heat and being woken up abruptly. She pointed upward. "The shades that were right there."

"Oh, those," Rita called from the open door where she clutched

23

an iced coffee in one hand. She stepped into the office, allowing Shadow to shuffle inside behind her before she continued using her free hand in a showy gesture meant to highlight her ombre manicure that featured different hues of the same color. "They were so tacky and plain. I threw them away."

"Plain or not, they helped keep the heat out when the sun hits the west-facing windows. You might appreciate that, especially come late afternoon when you'll be looking more like a wilted piece of celery with nothing to block the heat."

"I'm not worried." She waved away the comments. "There's no way I can look bad." Rita gazed at Tenny's sweat-stained shirt. "So sad," she sniffed. As if on cue, Shadow giggled. The two of them lounged on the red loveseat, alternatively sipping their cool drinks and loudly discussing the plans for the décor.

Tenny dropped a dictionary into a box slightly harder than she meant to while listening to the descriptions of the off-white interior and the possibility of Daddy Dearest putting in a high-end new car from the dealership into the reader room to bring in customers. Such an outrageous plan would mean the destruction of the wall, presently festooned with a *Cozy Summertime Reads* banner, to provide vehicle access. No thinking landlord would allow such an expensive proposition, but since the building owner called Rita daughter—it pretty much explained everything, including the library getting pushed out. The ownership topic may have never come up at the town council meeting. Tenny locked eyes with Connie. Without a word, she conveyed the need for urgency. Despite being past exhausted, they both picked up their speed.

Cinnamon used to tease her about her ability to block things out, especially when Tenny got engrossed in a riveting tale. She utilized this skill to ignore the continuing décor conversation until she heard Dallas' name. Clutching a popular paperback tighter than she needed, she maneuvered closer, put down the book, and grabbed at a banner to roll up in a less than subtle eavesdropping attempt.

"Ah, did you notice the way Dallas looked at me?" Rita asked her friend with a sly look, speaking loudly enough for the conversation to carry.

"Oh yeah." Shadow bobbed her head emphatically. "I bet he's kicking himself for letting you go."

"Who wouldn't?" Rita lifted one shoulder as if it were a given—at least in her mind. "Speak of the devil!" She pressed her hand against her chest. "As I live and breathe, the man can't stay away from me. It looks like he's brought me some goodies. Here!" She shoved the iced coffee at her lackey. "Take care of this."

Her friend picked up the drink and dropped it into the trash. Not wanting to see the sickening scene, Tenny moved toward the reading room center, but still caught sight of Dallas closing his truck door. He was not the skinny kid he used to be, but he still kept that gorgeous sun-streaked hair that most other men paid big bucks to duplicate.

The bell jangled and a languid, "Hello, Dallas!" floated from Rita, who no doubt struck a dramatic pose. "Fancy seeing you again."

"Uh, yeah." Dallas sounded uncomfortable—not a bit like a lovelorn male. "Hey, Tenny! Connie!"

The sound of their names resulted in both women turning and witnessing Dallas scurrying past the lounging Rita. He took three large steps and hurried through the office as if engaged in the childhood game of Escape from Burning Lava where you jump from furniture to furniture, as if avoiding said lava. The lava in this game semi-reclined on the red leather loveseat.

"Hey, y'all," Dallas announced in a cheery voice. "I brought you lunch. Heard from your hubby,"—he nodded to Connie—"that you two were slaving away through lunch."

"Bless you." Connie stepped forward and patted his arm. "Your mama did a good job with you."

He chuckled. "She tried." Dallas ducked his head at the compliment. He shook the bag. "*Sweet Beginnings* is now making lunch. Hope I got you all something you might like."

An appetizing scent of corned beef and the tang of sauerkraut scented the air, drawing Tenny closer. "You wouldn't have a Reuben sandwich in there, would you?"

He opened the bag, retrieved a foil-wrapped sandwich, and handed it to Tenny. "Check it out for yourself."

The aroma intensified as she unwrapped it, revealing a toasted rye bread sandwich stuffed with corned beef, melty Swiss cheese, and sauerkraut. "Oh my!" Her stomach growled, which made her laugh a tad self-consciously. "You have no clue how hungry I am. I missed breakfast because…" Her eyes went to the office area, and she left the statement unfinished, but Dallas nodded as if he understood. "Are you sure you're not my fairy godmother?"

"Ha ha!" He forced a laugh but grinned as he unloaded two large teas and a couple of cookies in wax paper bags. "I do my best. It would have helped if you'd called me and told me what you needed."

Not knowing how to reply, she took a bite of her sandwich, and then another. Dallas rested one hip against the table and talked while the two of them ate, catching her up on their shared friends from high school. In the background, she could hear Rita pacing and muttering, but refused to look at her. Finally, Rita announced, "Let's go! We have important stuff to do. I can't take the smell in this place. We need room deodorizers!"

A slamming door and angry bell jangle confirmed their exit. Connie's brow puckered as she cleared her throat. "Do you think she meant *us* when talking about the smell?"

"Nah," Dallas offered with an amused expression. "I think it may have been the Reubens. She never liked them. Claimed they were a messy, no-class sandwich. Refused to let me eat one in front of her. She said it offended her."

"Mmmm." Tenny hummed her reply but put away the possibility that somehow Dallas had remembered she loved Reubens. In their senior yearbook, they had silly questions they had to answer and she mentioned a good Reuben would be a perfect last meal. "So, you got the Reubens just to honk Rita off?"

"Nope." He turned and glanced at the closed door and empty parking space in front of it. "That was just a bonus." When he rocked back on his heels, he pointed to what little was left of the sandwich. "Good?"

"You have no clue." She held up the Reuben. "You want a bite?"

He accepted the offered sandwich and managed a small nibble. "Oh..." He hummed the word and his eyes rolled upward. "Delicious. I should have bought one of my own."

"Take it," she felt compelled to say—even though she wanted to gobble the rest of it like a starving alley cat.

"No." He handed the sandwich back to her with a grin. "I know good manners when I hear them. Finish your sandwich, but I might take half of your cookie."

Tenny opened the wrapped cookie and noticed that it, too, like the sandwich, was one of her favorites—peanut butter. "Peanut butter was always my favorite. How did you know?"

"You entered something involving peanut butter every year at the county fair. If it wasn't cookies, you worked peanut butter into whatever class you exhibited in," he reminded her in a genial tone, pulling a laugh from Connie.

"Oh mercy. I do remember your aunt trying to talk you out of the peanut butter cornbread."

The mention brought back the memory of the judges' confused faces as they bit into cornbread and discovered a texture and flavor they didn't expect. "Not my finest moment. I didn't even place. However, my peanut butter muffins took a blue ribbon. The chocolate peanut butter streusel coffee cake took home a grand championship."

For a few minutes, they discussed past fair memories; then Tenny recalled she had a job to do, which needed to be completed before the original mean girl came back. "It's been fun, but I need to pack up these books."

"I understand." Dallas stood and stuck his hands into the back pockets of his jeans. "I should get back to work, too."

"Oh?" Tenny glanced back at Dallas. "I remember how crazy you were about all living creatures. Are you running an animal shelter?" Considering how he nursed homeless wildlife in his youth, he'd be a natural choice for an animal shelter or rehab facility.

"Oh, no." He grinned, causing the sun lines around his eyes to crinkle. "While I do have a dog, a couple barn cats, and a goat, it doesn't qualify as a shelter. Spent a couple of years working in the city as an actuary. Money was good, but being inside all day long got old fast. I bought the Foster farm and am converting it into an organic farm. My first crop is sunflowers. You should come by and see it. Some are already blooming."

"Sounds beautiful."

"It is." He held up his hand, turning and leaving with a lightness in his step. The sun glinted on his blond hair as he climbed into his dirt-spattered pickup truck.

Connie sighed. "It's easy to see why Rita had her eye on him. Together, they looked like Malibu Barbie and Ken. I never could understand what he saw in her."

"The obvious."

"Oh no!" Connie insisted, standing and placing one hand on her hip. "He's a smart boy and had to know evil goes clear through that girl." She wagged her finger at Tenny. "Rumors are already flying about his behavior at the funeral. He's made his intentions clear. He has his eye on you."

"You're wrong!" Tenny wiped her hands on the napkin and picked up the remnants of her lunch. "He could have any single female in town."

"Technically, he could. However, most thinking females would steer clear of him. Rita's already put out *hands-off Dallas* messages since the two of them are getting back together some day."

"Huh." Her hands went back to massage the small of her back. "That sounds like Rita. Unfortunately, she forgot to say anything to Dallas."

"Maybe so." Connie sipped her tea before continuing, "What I do know is she'll make trouble for you if you stay and she thinks Dallas is sweet on you."

She held out her hands, palms up, as if the truth were self-evident. "I have no plans to get involved with Dallas. He's just an old friend."

"Uh-huh." Connie's disbelief coated the syllables. "Are you planning to stay with your aunt being gone?"

"It's too soon to tell."

Chapter Five

THE RED LIQUID in the outside thermometer stretched upwards toward a hundred. On extreme heat days like today, a young Tenny would have sat on the porch and stared at the thermometer, hoping for a cartoon reaction where it broke free of its glass container, spurting everywhere. It never happened. Just like steam never shot out of her ears when angry. If any possibility existed of her roaring like a hot kettle, it should have happened today with all the digs Rita landed.

The sound of another book box landing on the porch drew her attention to Henry, Connie's husband. The husky man sighed heavily, drew a bandana from his pocket, and ran it over his sweating bald dome. He managed a smile that created even more lines in his seamed face. Henry cocked one shaggy eyebrow and asked, "Hot enough for you?"

Somehow, she knew he'd say that because it served as his go-to line in the summer months. "Oh, no." She shook her head and fell into the easy banter from earlier years. "It's almost cool." They both laughed about the time Connie mounted the stairs, carrying a smaller book box. She clicked her tongue and asked, "Not the hot enough line?"

"You guessed it," Tenny replied, glancing at the box in Connie's arms. "Last one?" She took it and placed it beside the others waiting on the shaded front porch.

"It is." Connie put her hands on her hips, encased in floral capris, and gave a twist to one side, and then another. "I keep saying I need to exercise more. Just didn't expect to do it all in one day."

Knowing how weary she felt, Tenny could only imagine how tired Connie and Henry must be. Her stomach clenched a little. It could be hunger or guilt over having the two helpful seniors labor on the hottest day of the year so far. "Oh my goodness. Come inside. I have a pitcher of cold lemonade. Plenty of food, too. I can make you up a nice supper. Don't know where my manners are."

"Don't fuss," Connie advised as she wiggled her shoulders, stretching her joined hands over her head. "We need to get going anyway."

Henry cleared his throat before adding in a jovial tone, "Speak for yourself, woman. I never pass up lemonade. Might even take something sweet to balance it out." He held up his index finger. "I'll make you a deal. I'll bring the boxes inside—work for my treat, so to speak."

"Sounds good to me," Tenny agreed and placed her hand on the doorknob that turned easily under her hand. Half the time she locked the door, feeling somewhat more secure, but Aunt Cinnamon complained she didn't want to live somewhere that required locking doors. Out of deference to her aunt, she made a point of locking the door only after her aunt retired. However, this required her to get up early to unlock it, too. Her time away at college taught her not everyone had her best interest at heart, but she had known that before she left.

The three of them retired to the sunroom crowded with her

aunt's hanging spider plants with dangling baby plants, bushy Boston ferns, and one nameless purple striped vine. A square Formica table featured a bacon and eggs design worn away in spots where arms had rested as opposed to plates. Many a Euchre game had happened around the table. Chatter flowed as they sipped their lemonade and polished off thick slabs of pineapple upside-down cake. After a while, Connie nudged her husband, who acted surprised, and then nodded. "Well now, we'd better get going. Barney, our dog, will be wanting her dinner."

"Understandable," Tenny offered, wondering just how old Barney was. They'd always had a dog named Barney—a combination hound that if you closed one eye and squinted, you'd call him a basset hound. Do it with the other eye, and he'd be a beagle. "That dog still alive?"

"The one we have now is." Connie stood and picked up her empty plate. "This is our third dog named Barney. Thought we'd name the last one something else being female and all, but every time we went to call the pup, *Barney* just came out. Turns out it's the old human that's hard to teach new tricks." She peered down at the floor as if searching for something. "No Precious?"

"No." Tenny wrinkled her nose. If ever a creature didn't live up to its name, it would be Precious. Uncle Mark had found the homeless raccoon kit half-starved alongside the main road, and Aunt Cinnamon swooped into action, bottle feeding it and carrying it around swaddled in a second-hand baby blanket. Maybe she went overboard, but since it had happened after Tenny left, it helped her aunt with the transition. It was a little bothersome that an opportunistic animal could replace her. "That raccoon took off about the same time as Aunt Cinnamon decided to die at home. It bothered her that he didn't hang around, but she accepted that animals weren't usually ones for long goodbyes. He hasn't been back since.

A snort and a grumble came from Henry. "More likely he took off in search of a ladylove. Bet you a dollar he'll be back."

"I doubt it." Her nose crinkled as she considered the pampered animal. "He loved my aunt. After all, she'd fix him scrambled eggs with cheese every day. Me, he just tolerated. Could be because I never cooked for him." Her shoulders went up in a shrug. "How long do raccoons live anyhow? Precious has to be seven."

"Around seven, I assume." Henry agreed, sucking in his lips as his eyes briefly rolled upward. "Out in the wild, coons don't live long. Two, maybe three years. Most end up dead on the road." He winked, his face crinkling as he continued, "I heard those kept in captivity can live up to twenty years. My friend, Bud, kept one going for twenty-two years. In the end, he carried the deaf and blind raccoon on a pillow. I figure since you're the only heir, you now get Precious."

Tenny stuck out her tongue. "Not funny. I'm way too tired to hear any more about my aunt's favorite pet."

A chorus of laughter greeted her remark as the three of them made their way to the front door and said their goodbyes. The weight of the day slid from her shoulders as she closed the door and leaned against it. Delicate heads of the porcelain and crystal horses that her aunt collected showed over the stacked boxes, giving the appearance of being awash in a cardboard sea. Something about boxes gave the place an unsettling vibe. An unpacked carton could indicate a new adventure or one ending. Her lips pressed together as she tried to decide which one applied. Her initial plan revolved around taking care of her aunt. That's as far as she allowed herself to

BULLIES, BOVINES AND A BOOKMOBILE

think—not even dwelling on the inevitable end. A long sigh sounded as Tenny sank down onto the couch, only to realize she'd need her laptop. With a groan, she hauled herself up and went in search of her computer, which played a masterful game of hide-and-seek with her. Finally, she found it draped under her unmade bed covers.

On the way back to the living room, she noticed the lack of sound. There was no noise drifting in from parents calling their children home, no barking dogs, or a confused rooster who crowed at every hour except when he should. Rather eerie, it made her wonder how many times had she truly experienced silence? One too many, she decided and, locating the remote, powered on the television. An old sitcom provided the backdrop with shrill canned laughter—she lowered the volume until it resembled people talking in another room. It was restful in its own way. Tenny settled into the sea of throw pillows and booted up her computer, ready to wade through the remnants of her previous life.

The number of emails made her swallow hard, but with any luck, most would be spam. All she had to do was narrow down what was worth reading and delete the rest. Her eyes passed over various charities asking for her help to save the whales, the butterflies, homeless dogs and cats, and plenty of organizations for librarians begging her to join—for a price. A familiar name stopped her scrolling. Darlena, her old boss back at the university—whom she could picture with her half-moon glasses held by a decorative chain around her neck. The woman owned the image of a head librarian with her tweed suits and low bun hairstyle. Most of the students avoided her, unaware of how incredibly witty and kind she could be. The prospect of a letter delighted her—a voice from another world, in a manner of speaking.

Dear Tenny,

I saw your aunt's obituary. You have my sincere condolences. I know this has been a long, painful road for you. Your aunt was lucky to have you. I know it will take time to get things settled, but I thought it wouldn't hurt to give you something to think about.

Noreen, the woman I hired to fill in for you, is going to take pregnancy leave soon. She's expecting to be gone six months or more. Often, young mothers don't always come back. It goes without saying, I'd love to have you back.

Chapter Six

THE SCENT OF Cinnamon's vanilla body wash lingered in the bathroom. Tenny stared at herself in the mirror as she brushed her teeth. Near the corner of the mirror, a taped index card announced *Make the Best of the Day*. Every single thing in the house reminded her of her aunt and uncle. That was no big surprise, since it was their house, crammed with their stuff and memories. She snorted at her not-so-clever realization and ended up choking on the toothpaste suds. After spitting it out, she met her eyes in the mirror. Her reflective self, she swore, raised an eyebrow, possibly even questioning Tenny's ability to handle the current situation. It was pretty bad when your own reflection demonstrated doubt.

Barefoot, she padded out of the bathroom and headed for her bed, past ready to dissolve into dreamland. She clicked off the lights behind her, progressing to her childhood bedroom—her aunt kept it the way she had left it. Instead of being papered in posters of attractive male celebrities grinning at the camera, she'd chosen a half-dozen slightly out-of-focus nature photos with poems written across them in flowing script. The one with the horse standing at the fence on a snowy evening pulled her back to ninth grade when she thumb-tacked it to the wall, having more than a little crush on their newly minted English teacher, who most of the girls referred to as

Heathcliff, as in *Wuthering Heights*, because of his dark, brooding good looks. The name indicated they, like the heroine, would be willing to do irrational acts to be close to him. Tenny, not immune to an excellent reading voice or soulful eyes, wrote rambling poems chock-full of metaphors, hoping to impress her crush. Her nose crinkled at her former antics. If nothing else, it gave her a greater appreciation for legitimate poets.

She flicked on the bedside lamp before turning off the ceiling fixture. The small hobnailed lamp threw a decent circle of illumination, giving sufficient light to read. In her aunt's world, that's how you measured a light. *No reading tonight*, Tenny promised herself as she slid between the cool percale sheets smelling slightly of starch. Her aunt stocked the linen closet with ironed sheets, calling it a labor of love. Her fingers slid along the fabric surface, knowing it would be her last encounter with pressed bedclothes.

Thinking she might as well get to sleep, her hand hovered in the air near the lamp switch as if it encountered a barrier preventing her from turning off the light. Normally, she slept with the light off. Maybe she would leave it on—just for tonight. A couple of half-hearted turns and punches to the pillow failed to build the appropriate architecture of limbs and pillows she needed to sleep. Flopping onto her back, she laced her hands under her head and stared up at the ceiling. A brown discoloration near the corner hinted at a leak in the roof she'd have to investigate. It didn't matter if she stayed or sold the house—no one wanted a leaky roof. What would her life be like if she returned to the city?

Darlena hinted at her old job, but truthfully, Noreen wouldn't lose her position for taking pregnancy leave. Her lips twisted as she considered the situation. All would be good until Noreen wanted to come back, and then Tenny would step down, possibly taking a circulation assistant job, performing the same duties she did as a student. All the same, no one said she *had* to go back to her old job. University libraries dotted the map, and many needed experienced librarians. Public librarians made much less than university ones did. Some barely eked out minimum wage. In those cases, the job usually served as something to do during retirement to supplement their income.

Blue's talk about buying a bus and starting a bookmobile tantalized her for a moment or two, especially when she thought about how pleased Cinnamon would be. There were a few issues with the scenario, with the main one being she had no clue what went into running a bookmobile. Then again, the money she would need to raise served as a major stumbling block. She inhaled audibly, considering her aunt's declaration that she'd put aside some money for Tenny and her legacy. The way her aunt ran the words together in her pain-killer induced haze made her question if Tenny and legacy were two separate things or if Tenny should *be* the legacy.

A rustling in the lilac bushes outside her bedroom window interrupted her musing. Turning toward the noise, as if the action would somehow increase her ability to sense whatever scurried through the bush as if she possessed X-ray vision, she waited for another sound. Back in the city, she'd already be reaching for her can of roach spray, which her college roommate assured her served as well as mace for half the cost.

Despite residing on Main Street, bunnies and possums often found their way into yards, sometimes nibbling on food put out for pets. To distract herself, Tenny reached for her phone and scrolled through the messages. There weren't too many recent ones—she kept going back in time, seeing how far she needed to go before she found Andrew's name, her on-again, off-again boyfriend. *Two months.* With everything in her life, she hadn't even noticed his absence. Apparently, they were in an off-again phase. He didn't even earn a mention to Blue. Her aunt insisted Tenny deserved better treatment, and on that point, they could agree.

A scratching noise joined the rustling sound, sending a shiver up her back. She set her chin, her shoulders tensing as she slowly slipped from the bed, inching to the window. It was probably nothing. At worst, it could be kids engaged in an after-dark game of hide-and-seek. A wistful smile crossed her face, remembering the times she'd played Red Rover or Capture the Flag with the neighborhood children. Somehow, when the sun started to wane, the games took an exciting turn when played after dusk. Satisfied with her explanation, her shoulders relaxed and she moved back toward the waiting bed when a loud crash came from outside.

It could have been one of the many flower pots filled with blooming plants scattered all over the yard. Salvia, sedum, and echinacea filled the side yards. Besides the in-ground plants, containers of different shapes and sizes filled the back yard, which resulted in lots of watering. Cinnamon started this process decades ago, growing blossoms for a friend's outdoor wedding. Soon, others started asking to borrow certain plants for events, parties, church, and weddings. It served as an endowment for the community, especially when the perennials weathered inside, crowding every surface and vying for window space.

Her eyes narrowed as she fisted her hands. Whoever was out there had demolished one of her aunt's beloved plants. Not cool. An errant memory of one of the funeral visitors lamenting about

Tenny's being all alone in the house before offering up her failure-to-launch son as the solution came to mind. *Good grief!* Did they think they'd scare her into tying the knot?

Also, were they unaware she helped Blue move the dairy herd to a new pasture in the next county only using a clothesline? She even helped Uncle Mark capture an aging mountain lion that escaped from the nearby exotic feline rescue sanctuary. No clumsy bachelor would frighten her or get his hands on her inheritance. She turned off the lamp and waited a few seconds to allow her eyesight to grow accustomed to the dark before moving soundlessly toward the partially open window, covered only by a thin screen.

A crescent moon, along with a security light mounted on the garage, threw out shadows but still gave shape to things—the clothesline, the metal patio table, and the garden wagon she'd forgotten to put away. Nothing out of place or human sized resided near the sides of the detached garage. Nearby, a metal screen door slammed, causing her to jump. Hiding in the dark and peering out the window, pretty soon the kids would start making up stories about her. Would they warn each other not to be lured into the house and forced to read a "classic" book, or would it be something a tad more sinister?

Something slapped the screen only inches from her face, causing her to stumble back while swallowing a startled cry. Her hand pressed against her chest, trying to still her racing heart. Two dark, accusing eyes glared at her, judging her. Tenny caught her breath and then spat out the name of her surprise visitor. "Precious!"

Chapter Seven

SUN STREAMED IN through the parted ruffled curtains. The radio on the kitchen counter played a country ballad about a man who lost the great loves of his life when his cheated-on girlfriend drove off in his truck with his blue tick hound. Tenny tried to join in on the chorus as she scrambled eggs in the skillet. Her unfamiliarity with the song caused her to go up high when the singer went low. Outside her back screen door, a familiar voice asked, "Is someone in pain, or is that just you singing?"

Leave it to Blue to tell it like it is. "C'mon in. You know it's me."

Her friend clopped in wearing her rubber muck boots, jeans, and a T-shirt that featured a cartoon Holstein with extra-long lashes. A ball cap emblazoned with the dairy's name, Moo Town, hid most of her blonde locks. As she entered, she nodded at the almost done eggs. "Didn't expect breakfast—especially since I never mentioned I was coming."

"I did wonder if you were expected," Tenny commented as she opened a cabinet to retrieve a stainless-steel bowl and scraped the finished eggs into it. When she placed the bowl on the floor, Precious scampered out from behind the large flower pots where he'd taken refuge. The raccoon cocked his head and gave Tenny an inquiring look.

"Okay," Tenny huffed and grabbed another bowl, filled it with water and placed it beside the egg bowl. Precious grabbed a paw full of eggs and dipped it into the water before popping it into his mouth.

Blue's eyebrows inched upward and her mouth dropped open as she watched the entire procedure. "Precious?" She stated the obvious. "I thought you hated him."

Putting one finger to her lips, she angled her head at the creature, stuffing his face. "Aunt Cinnamon loved him. I think he served as a surrogate child when I left for college. I imagine Precious is missing Aunt Cinnamon right now."

"Why wouldn't he? The woman babied him. She even decked out that stroller for him to ride in when it's perfectly obvious he can walk. And here you are cooking for him. Are you going to take over where Cinnamon left off?"

"No." Tenny gave an emphatic shake of her head and busied herself making her own breakfast of peanut butter toast. "I feel sorry for him, losing the only person who cared about him."

"That feeling will wear off once he trashes the house or ruins something you value. He's a wild creature, not some potential boyfriend who's rough around the edges. Decent haircut and clothes that aren't overalls could improve the rough-around-the-edges guy, but that won't work on Precious. He will always be a raccoon, engaging in things raccoons do, such as pawing through garbage."

"Oh, no. He won't be going through the garbage. I plan on feeding him. Aunt Cinnamon would expect that."

Blue cupped one hand around her ear. "Did you just hear yourself? The Tenny I know would lock the door to keep him out."

"He tore through the window screen," she added, facing away

from her friend, not wanting to observe her smirk.

"And yet you made him breakfast?"

Tenny shrugged and turned to address Blue. "It's not an every-day thing. I have a plan. Instead of his favorite meals, I'll make them a little less wonderful. Maybe too salty. Brown rice instead of white. Eventually, he'll be heading for the woods on his own."

Blue pushed her hat up and wrinkled her nose. "You realize you are talking about a critter that happily consumes garbage. I'm not sure you can even cook bad enough to make him leave."

Having finished his breakfast, Precious hopped onto a stool, using it to gain access to the counter. He casually strolled toward the table still filled with goodies brought by neighbors. Foil wrappers and snap-on lids served as no barrier to Precious' agile fingers. He lifted the cover on a German chocolate cake and took a swipe. A thoughtful expression crossed his face, as if considering tasting the cake without any water. Tenny flicked a dish towel at him. "Get! Get down."

He leapt to the floor, leaving a smear of chocolate on the linoleum before dashing for safety in another room. Other storage measures would be required with Precious in the house. Instead of commenting, Blue made do with one raised eyebrow that reiterated everything she had just mentioned.

"I know," Tenny muttered as she grabbed her toast and moved toward the table. "There's some coffee in the coffee maker. You can make yourself some toast, too."

"Coffee sounds good." Blue poured some into a cup with the slogan *Book Boyfriends are the Best* and joined Tenny at the table. "I didn't come for coffee." She paused to sip her brew. "All the same, I won't turn it down. We're finished with the morning milking." She mimed wiping the sweat off her brow. "Glad I can say that. So much has gone wrong this past year. We even had trouble with our milkers—the machines, not the girls. Replacing the machines could run three to nine hundred dollars, depending what we bought. Griffin decided to disassemble one and noticed the power line was broken. Half of the machines were broken. Much cheaper to fix them than to buy new.

"Anyhow…" Blue made a face. "Forget about the dairy. I thought it'd be an excellent time to go check out that bus I told you about. The owner, Shelley, is ready to head to Florida. She's heard all about pickleball, bingo on the beach, and canasta tournaments that go on until ten p.m. Since her hubby Isaac died and she officially retired from the post office, she can't wait to go wild. Even bought some of those tropical caftans with leaves and flowers. That means she's a motivated seller."

Tenny choked on her peanut butter toast and reached for her coffee. After swallowing a healthy swig, she audibly exhaled while turning the prospect of a bookmobile in her mind. Until now, it existed as a possibility—a faraway one, the way she might consider running a marathon and yet doing nothing to train for it. Still, what could it hurt to check it out? "How far away is the bus?"

A phone chirp had Blue pulling her cell out of her pocket instead of answering her inquiry. She stared at the message, the ends of her lips pulling down. She typed something and then explained. "Rupert is missing."

The way she said the name, Tenny felt as if she should recognize it, but she'd forgotten a great deal about the town's residents when she left. When she returned, she had tended to her aunt and the library. "Rupert, your…cousin?"

"Rascally Rupert," Blue explained with dancing eyes and a smirk. "You know? The gentleman bull."

"Oh yeah." An image of the sizable, but mainly black Holstein bull came to mind. Blue's husband was a trendsetter in the dairy industry by insisting on grass-fed cows and making raw milk cheeses. In other ways, he was a traditionalist, demonstrated by keeping an actual bull. Other farms went with artificial insemination. "I remember him. We called him king of his pasture since you kept him away from the other cows."

"Most of the time," Blue agreed with a nod. She stood and ventured over to the covered goodies, browsed, selected an oatmeal cookie, and returned to the table. "As you know, it takes almost ten months for a bovine pregnancy, so we need to start now for spring calves. With that in mind, we were going to bring in Rupert to introduce him to his latest girlfriends." Her brow furrowed, and she shook her head slowly. "He's not in the east field."

Knowing a prize-winning bull like Rupert could easily cost up to six figures, Tenny knew such a loss would endanger their entire dairy operation. "Maybe you should go home and help look for him."

Blue forced a laugh. "I'm not worried. Last time, he forced down the fence and got into Demings' cornfield. They were quick to call us." She shrugged. "It's probably something like that. Rupert gets bored alone. He needs a friend. Maybe we could get him a goat. I hear they use goats with racehorses to keep them calm."

"Maybe," Tenny said, polishing off her toast and carrying the plate to the sink. "Let's go look at the bus. Then you can get back to looking for your missing bull."

"I'm not worried."

"You forgot to tell your face that."

"Oh." Blue's fingers touched her brow and temple as if she could shape it into a less anxious expression. "Well, maybe a little worried. The dairy business has its ups and downs. Currently, we're in a down. Rupert's out-of-town girlfriends help pay the bills and allow us little luxuries, such as the industrial fridge for our dairy shop products."

"No local dairy farmers use Rupert's services?"

"Ha!" Despite her forced laugh, Blue stuck her tongue out, which served as her go-to response ever since first grade when someone said something silly. "That would mean acknowledging our Rupert is the better bull. We already know that. Still, we have our rivals."

"Darling Dairy?"

"No. They're a high-yield commercial dairy that shoot up their girls with hormones to milk them three times a day. They don't use actual bulls. Williams Dairy or Appleton's are the most likely rivals—farms about the same size, using similar methods, and the owners are around my husband's age."

"You don't think either one of them would steal Rupert?"

Blue inhaled and worked her chin one way, then another. "Nah. There's honor among dairy farmers. When I mentioned Moo Town being in a slump, I meant the price of milk. Occasionally, family dairies help one another when the need arises." She pointed to Tenny. "We can go as soon as you take care of your masked visitor."

"You're right." A crash sounded in the distance, causing her to cringe. "I think I know where Precious is."

As she hurried off to discover what chaos her wildlife guest had rained upon the household, Blue called after her. "I'll close all the windows to prevent any return visits while we're gone!"

Chapter Eight

TENNY CLIMBED INTO the white pickup liberally coated with randomly shaped black spots to resemble a Holstein. Moo Town's number and email were listed in block printing on the doors and truck gate. Since Blue knew where the bus owner lived, it made more sense to let her drive. She flipped down the sun visor, dimming the intense sun only a little. Somehow, in the city, Tenny forgot how unrelenting the summer heat could be in Emerson without any convenient tall buildings creating shade. Using her flattened hand as a sun shield, she glanced back at the house. Precious stood on his hind legs with one front paw reaching for the front doorknob. "You locked all the windows, right?"

"Yep," Blue answered and pulled the driver's door shut, waiting for Tenny to do likewise before starting the truck. "I know Precious can be annoying, but I doubt he can pry open a locked window."

"You'd think that." She kept her eyes on the resourceful raccoon as the truck shifted into drive. "Let's make this trip as fast as possible. You need to help look for Rupert, and I need to get back to guarding against my own personal break-in artist, or maybe just feed him lunch."

"Sweetie, be strong. There's no clause in the will that you have to take care of Precious, or is there?"

Her lips pressed together and her eyes rolled up as she tried to recall any conversations with her aunt regarding this. She tucked a curl that escaped from the loose topknot behind her ear as she answered. "I don't think so. Quite frankly, I have no clue what was in the will. Before Uncle Mark died, I served as a witness to their original wills, but after his death, a new will was made." Her shoulders went up in a shrug. "For all I know, Aunt Cinnamon left everything to Precious. For all those mamas trying to interest me in their sons, they might change their tune if they find out I received nothing. Then again, I have no clue how much money they had. Looking back over the years, they certainly never lived a rich life. The two family vacations we took were road trips to Branson, Missouri, and the Smoky Mountains."

"You know…" Blue turned her head, grinned, and then turned back to watch the road as she spoke "…it might be a real joke if you married one of those fellows and then revealed that you had nothing." Her laughter punctuated the statement.

"Funny for you!" Tenny shook her head hard. "I'm not getting married just so you can laugh your head off."

"Fair enough." Blue flicked on her blinker and took a right turn onto a gravel road. "Our bus owner lives off the beaten path, which means you might want to roll up your window or suck in a lot of dust. Personally, I could do without the dust."

The truck hit a pothole, causing both women to bounce. "Could you try to not hit each hole?"

"It's hard since the road is mainly holes. It needs more gravel. City living has made you soft," Blue teased.

"No, it hasn't. I've never liked being slung around like a watermelon in the back of a truck bed. Besides, there are different problems in the city."

"Like what? Not getting your soy latte on time?"

"No problem getting soy lattes, but I prefer regular milk lattes."

"As you should."

"Parking can be an issue since most places don't provide it. Often when I came home at night my parking space was gone. I would have to park blocks away from my apartment. Not cool since I wouldn't be able to see my car. In the winter, I'd dig out a space for my vehicle in the morning, only to have some opportunistic jerk snatch it."

Blue snorted. "Bad deal. No manners. Anything else?"

"There's not a wealth of decent guys. Everyone I met who seemed nice was already in a relationship."

"I hate when that happens. Good thing I grabbed my hunk of burning love early."

"You're the lucky one."

"That I am." Blue chuckled. "You know, the weird thing is, before Griffin and I became an item, guys had zero interest in little ol' me. I was just some chunky blonde. A few older folks even made comments about how I looked like the Campbell's soup girl. That's back when advertisers were okay with using plump people. I think it symbolized jolly or something." Her lips twisted, she coughed, and continued, "A weird thing happened after we became a couple. Not sure if I ever mentioned it. Personally, I wasn't a hundred percent sure it even happened."

Curious about the *something* Blue may or may not have told her, Tenny reached across the seat to poke her friend. "Enough build up. Spill it."

"You remember Randall from fifth grade?"

A memory of a skinny kid with thick glasses who had the habit of wiping his nose on his T-shirt came to mind. "Sort of…"

"Well, Randall prefers to be called Rand now. After I started hanging out with my sweetie, he sees Griffin at the hardware store and tells him he better treat me right. Weird, huh?"

"Sounds like a crush to me."

"Yeah, I thought so, too. Despite living in a small town, I almost never saw Rand. When I did, I would say 'Hey' just like I would with anyone else. My point is men tend to find you interesting when you're already involved with someone. Maybe it's because you're unavailable. Forbidden fruit or something."

The ridiculousness of it all forced a snort out of Tenny. "It could be guys don't know what they want."

"There's that," Blue granted with a nod. "Speaking of men possibly not knowing what they want, what about the guy your aunt mentioned you were dating?"

"Geesh!" An audible exhale escaped her. Just when she thought her sometime boyfriend served as her personal secret, it wasn't. A mental image of her beloved aunt telling everyone that her girl had a beau made her slump against the seat. "Did she tell everyone?"

"I'm not everyone." Blue protested. "You somehow forgot to mention it when you came back. I kept waiting, but nothing." Her nose crinkled. "It made me think maybe that relationship crashed and burned."

"You're not too far off. Crashing and burning makes it sound grander than it actually was. We'd date for a while, then we wouldn't. No grand passion. No future plans. Mainly, he stopped calling me, and I stopped caring."

"You're right. So not grand and blander than anything else.

Forget about him." She cleared her throat and declared dramatically, "Madame Blue predicts major developments in your future."

"Hmm, not sure if I could handle any more major developments. How about a tall, dark, handsome man or fame? Not sure you'd get many repeat customers as a fortune teller," she commented as the gravel road turned into a dirt road, raising choking dust clouds. Even though the windows were closed, dust seeped in through the vents, irritating her sinuses. A swig from the water bottle cleared her throat, and the dust clouds dissipated enough to see a neat log cabin with a front garden composed of zinnias and wildflowers.

"Madame Blue can only say what she sees and nothing more." Returning to her normal voice, she said, "We're here." She waved in the direction of the cabin. "You're going to love the bus. Word is the Rise and Shine church ladies' group is after it, too. They want it for a party bus."

"Party bus?" She echoed the words with a tinge of disbelief.

"Oh yeah. Some conversion will be needed to put a round card table in it with swivel chairs and a fridge for their refreshments. They're planning on playing hearts and Uno all the way to the quilt show or their monthly musical theater luncheon. Right now, they have to carpool."

The possibility of competing against another buyer worried her. She hadn't even googled what used short buses should cost. Her hand slipped to the back of her neck and rubbed. If this was something her aunt would love, she should do it. Even so, it didn't sound like a project that would make money. Instead, it would probably drain any money she had—and she'd have to park the bookmobile when she had no more funds. It could turn out to be a huge white elephant she'd have to sell down the road. Maybe she could get local towns to pay a service fee to have the bookmobile services—that seemed fair. Maybe other burgs would be more open to residents reading—especially when they didn't have Rita's father pushing his own agenda.

Ambivalent if the bookmobile thing would even work, she worried her bottom lip with her teeth as Blue parked. Her companion possessed enough enthusiasm for the two of them. They both slipped from the truck with Blue chatting as they did so. "Let me do the talking. Skoolie fans are buying up retired school buses right and left. They can usually get them for between three thousand and six thousand, depending on the age of the bus and the condition of the engine. Diesel engines tend to last a long time if maintained properly."

Tenny shot her friend a surprised look. "Skoolie? You even know the lingo. Should I ask what a skoolie is?"

"Converted school bus. Besides bookmobiles, they can be converted into tiny homes and luxury campers. The real expense is in the conversion."

A slender woman dressed in a red gingham dress opened the door and waved. Initially, Tenny thought it couldn't be Shelley because she looked too young, but on closer inspection, the platinum blonde hair turned out to be white. A wide smile emphasized the lines time had etched on her face.

Shelley clapped her hands together. "I hope you're here to buy my bus. The ocean's been calling my name and my feet are itching to be gone."

Not sure what to say, Tenny waited for Blue to respond, who did in a somber tone, unlike her regular cheery manner. "Depends. Let's see it first. Then we'll talk."

"Absolutely," Shelley agreed and gestured to the back of the house where an open barn stood. "I've kept it in the barn. Babied it. Kept it clean. You could eat off the seats." She giggled as if the possibility amused her.

"Sounds good so far. How old is it?" Blue continued in her serious mien.

"Twenty years." The woman patted her own cheek. "Don't let that scare you. She doesn't show her age like me. No one would guess I'm sixty-two."

Again, not knowing if she should respond or not, Tenny glanced at Blue, who gave a small shake of the head. They entered a dimly lit barn where a short yellow bus waited. As far as Tenny could tell, it *looked* like a bus. Curiosity caused her to forget Blue's instructions. "Do all bus drivers have to buy their own buses?"

"Oh, no." Shelley put both hands on her hips and puffed out her chest a little. "Only the smart ones do. The post office has limited hours. It allowed me to not only do the regular bus route but also field trips and sports runs. A normal bus driver gets very little for those excursions since most of it goes into the school's pocket. As an independent driver, I get the entire fee, but it also means I fuel up my own vehicle, which is why I have a short bus instead of a full-size one. Quite frankly, short buses are easier to drive and fewer kids. Want to see inside?"

It made sense to peer inside and get a feel for the space. When no answer sounded, Tenny glanced at Blue, who was staring at her phone with a furrowed brow. Obviously, something had happened, so it was up to Tenny to carry on the negotiations with her nonexistent bankroll. "Sure. Let's take a look inside."

The door creaked open and Shelley motioned for Tenny to go

first. A slight antiseptic smell permeated the bus, demonstrating the clean factor. The green vinyl seats had high padded backs just in case of sudden stops. A slow turn allowed her to take in the entire bus, including the exit door in the back, which would allow for a comfortable traffic flow of bookmobile patrons. It wouldn't hold a ton of books, but right now they didn't *have* a ton of books. Best of all, it might be easier to park than a full-size bus. "Automatic?"

"I wouldn't have it any other way. Most of your school buses are automatic. It's hard enough to drive a bus full of screaming kids and then have to deal with a stick shift, too."

So far, it sounded good. Tenny exited the bus and imagined the exterior painted with an eye-catching turquoise with *Bookmobile* in multi-colored letters. Blue, still staring at her phone, asked, "What about the accident?"

The smile slipped from Shelley's face and she sniffed. "I swear that Marla runs her mouth. It was just a little accident. Nothing big. These things happen. Nothing to damage the frame."

That *could* be true. Fender benders happen all the time, maybe more when your fender takes up more space on the road. To Tenny, it wasn't a deal breaker. She could already see herself driving the bus to the next town, wearing one of her book-centric shirts, the radio playing, on her way to open doors for new and older readers alike.

"Price?" Blue inquired and lifted her head to make eye contact.

"Twenty-two thousand."

Blue brandished her phone. "According to the Internet, a twenty-year-old short bus in primo condition shouldn't be more than ten thousand dollars. I suspect yours has issues a wax job can't hide. Good luck selling it."

For many that would be the end of the bickering, but Shelley desperately needed to be in Florida and Tenny needed a bus.

Chapter Nine

THE WOMEN STOOD in the shadow of the open barn after checking out the short bus for sale. A confused rooster crowed in the distance, and clouds scudded over the sun, dimming the day for a few seconds—long enough for Blue to narrow her eyes, shove the phone into her pocket, and stomp off toward her truck muttering, leaving Tenny behind to speak to the openmouthed Shelley.

"Um…" Tenny stalled, smoothing her hands down the front of her pants. Having never engaged in bus negotiation, the proper protocol eluded her, but it probably didn't include stomping off. "I appreciate you showing us the bus. We'll keep in touch." She held up her hand and finger-waved but felt she needed something else to cover for her friend's rudeness. "Have fun in Florida."

Not waiting for a reply, she sprinted to the truck, which had already rumbled to life. "Hey!" Tenny exclaimed as she swung open the door, almost afraid Blue had forgotten she'd even arrived with her. "Glad you didn't take off without me."

No sooner had her posterior hit the vinyl than the truck jerked into motion, forcing Tenny to grab the door and shut it. After fastening her seatbelt, she glanced at a tight-lipped Blue, who stared straight ahead. "Okay," Tenny said, "twenty-two thousand was way out of the ballpark, but maybe she wanted to dicker."

"Nope." Blue grunted the word. "She wanted you to finance her fun in the sun. So many things wrong with that scenario."

"Besides the price?" Which served as the major obstacle, in her opinion.

"Showing us the bus in a dim barn? If she had nothing to hide, it would be in the sunlight. She never offered to let you drive it. Didn't even bother to start it up or even show us the engine."

Everything Blue said made sense. "You're right. I should have at least tried to drive it. Maybe it's just as well, since I have no clue if I even have the money to buy it. First, I need to talk to Wendall Duncan, my aunt's attorney." None of what she said had any effect on a grim-faced Blue, who clutched the steering wheel so hard her knuckles whitened. "Hey, I know you want the bookmobile idea to work, but there have to be other used school buses for sale. What's *really* wrong?"

Blue exhaled hard and loosened her grip on the steering wheel a little. "I got a text while you were checking out the bus interior."

"And?" Tenny prompted.

"The gate where we keep Rupert was unlatched."

"Could he have unlatched it?" She'd heard plenty of complaints about horses unlocking stall gates and barn doors. Surely bulls could do the same.

"He never has before. While he's maybe the gentleman bull, no one has ever called him smart. Griffin jokes he's all brawn and no brain."

"You did say he was bored. Maybe he's been practicing. Were there hoof marks?"

The truck slowed as Blue took her foot off the gas to consider. "He didn't say. Just texted Blue wasn't in the Demings' field and the gate was open. It should be easy to follow hoofprints. It hasn't rained for a while, which could have made Rupert anxious for greener grass. We should go check it out. Remember when we created the mystery club?"

"Yeah." When they were about ten, Uncle Mark caught the two of them using the garden hose to make the basement into a swimming pool. Rather than rage about the damage and mess, he deduced they were bored children in need of an activity. He started them on mystery solving, with the original missions involving finding things he'd hidden. The last bit of info she learned about recently from her aunt. "I'm not sure if our mystery skills are up to finding Rupert."

Silence filled the cab as they bumped down the road while whacking one particularly large pothole very hard. Tenny grabbed the dashboard. "Ah, Blue…I'd love to go check out the field with you. I'm just not certain what we could do that the guys aren't doing already."

"Different perspective, ya know. People see what people want to see. Surely you've read enough mysteries and watched enough crime dramas to know that. Whenever someone is arrested for bilking widows out of their life savings or setting the local VFW on fire, a reporter shows up and asks the neighbors about the convicted felon. Most of them say what a nice guy he was or how he kept to himself, as if hiding in your house is a good thing. However," she raised her voice, "there's usually a woman who mentions that she never trusted the guy, or her dog disliked him or something like that. It's because she looked at him differently. Maybe she didn't accept keeps-to-himself as being a good thing, or maybe she trusted her dog. All I know is we have to try." Her voice wavered on the last word.

When it came to mysteries, Tenny devoured Sherlock Holmes, Agatha Christie, and Ngaio Marsh. She even read the translated Umberto Eco tales. However, most readers take a break and watch television now and then. She preferred the quirky detective Monk while her aunt remained a lifelong Jessica Fletcher fan when she wasn't working her way through cozies filled with recipes. Often, the two of them would compete to solve the crime before the television sleuth did. Usually, they won. Still, that couldn't count for much, since writers probably planned it that way to keep viewers happy. Nevertheless, she'd risk being bitten by chiggers or swarmed by gnats for her bestie. "Maybe I should stop off and get my magnifying glass."

A honk behind them forced Blue into guiding the truck over to the side of the road as a black pickup passed them towing a horse trailer and stirring up dust. The trailer bounced and clattered as it went past. Blue leaned forward, peering out the windshield. "You don't see a bull in there, do you?"

"Nothing. Didn't you notice it bouncing all over the place? A bull must weigh around a thousand pounds."

"Closer to two thousand."

"My point is the trailer wouldn't bounce, and no way could the truck go that fast."

"You're right." Blue sighed, moved back onto the narrow road, steering close to the other side, slowed, and then peered at the yellow flowers that served as crop cover before bumping the truck into the field.

Suspecting that Blue's being upset about Rupert was clouding her judgment, Tenny shouted, "What are you doing? You're driving across a field! There have to be rules about that!" Her head swiveled left and right, expecting someone to dart out from the shadow of a nearby tree with a loaded shotgun.

"It's my cousin's property. He's letting it go fallow this year to build it up. It's the fastest way to get to 90N, which is the road to Moo Town."

Putting it like that *almost* made sense. The truck parted the flowers with a swishing sound. "This is much smoother than the road."

"Yeah, probably because no one uses the field."

Fifteen minutes later, they pulled up to a white post and rail fence. A sign identified the place as the *Home of Rupert, the Championship Holstein Bull.* While many farmers posted signs about what type of crop they grew, putting up a sign about your bull had to be similar. As far as she knew, no one stole a field of corn. Next to the sign stood a red-faced Griffin with his hair sticking up in tufts, probably from shooting his hands through it. From this angle, a bald spot in the back showed—not something she'd mention. Next to him, Dallas stood with a straw Stetson pushed back on his head. Even though she'd never considered Dallas as a farmer, he'd make a good spokesman for everything from tractors to chicken feed.

Focus, Tenny reminded herself. Somewhere out there, Rupert needed rescuing.

Chapter Ten

ANYONE DRIVING BY the post and rail white fence might assume that Griffin and Dallas were enjoying a nice visit in the middle of a sunny summer afternoon as opposed to trying to figure out the last location of a misplaced, expensive bull. In contrast to this peaceful scene, Blue gritted her teeth as she steered Moo Town's work truck toward the two conversing men, and then slammed on the brakes, parked the truck and jumped out, running to her husband, who opened his arms wide. The two of them embraced tightly while crying and whispering. This left Tenny awkwardly exiting the truck. Not knowing where to start on her bull-finding mission, she strolled over to Dallas, who leaned against the fence.

Small talk never featured in her skill set but completely deserted her with someone like Dallas—a decent, attractive fellow who'd been kind to her. She tucked her hands into the back pockets of her pants, trying for a casual effect. "You here to search for Rupert?"

He nodded. "Thought I'd lend a hand. I heard about it when I dropped by the feed and seed store. You know how gossip is in small towns."

Remembering her recent conversation about her aunt gossiping about her relationship with Andrew, she arched her eyebrows. "Believe me, I do."

His eyes danced with amusement. "I'm sure you do."

She angled her head to the conversing couple. "Any luck on Rupert?"

A heavy sigh served as the initial answer. "He's not in the Demings' cornfield. I drove the length of the field that faced the road. It's kind of hard to hide a Holstein of that size."

"Any clues?"

"Not really." He glanced over at the couple who had now separated and were speaking in normal voices. "Wish there were something else I could do. It's just weird. Sure, cows go off on their own, looking for greener pastures. Rupert probably did the same."

"Maybe." The earlier proposal of reviving the mystery club nudged her. Uncle Mark may have planted the items for them to find, but they were just kids then. As two grown adult women with multiple skill sets, maybe they *could* find Rupert. Instead, she said, "Now we'll have to wait for someone who's discovered Rupert in their rose garden munching on the blooms to call."

"I'd like to do—" Dallas stopped mid-sentence when his cell buzzed and withdrew his phone from his jeans pocket. His lips pulled down into a frown as he read the message. "Something's come up. I need to go. Can you make my goodbyes for me?"

"Sure," she agreed and watched him jog over to his truck parked in the shadows of two sizable elms. What would make him take off like that? Something urgent. Possibly his farm—after all, it served as his livelihood. It could be Rita, too. She wouldn't put it past the woman to create an emergency that required Dallas' assistance. Being the decent guy he was, he'd help. Connie hinted she might want to investigate why Dallas filed for divorce. She'd do that right after she located a runaway Rupert.

A half-dozen pickup trucks rumbled up onto the brittle grass, stopping near the fence. Men of various ages exited the vehicles, a few dressed in overalls, others in jeans, and one who had on cargo shorts as a nod to the hot weather—he must be the city slicker who'd spurred the most recent gossip. Rumors swirled around his electric car and working remotely. There was no electric car in evidence, so he must have hitched a ride. It was pretty decent of him to help look for Rupert. What she really wanted to know was how he got reliable Internet when half the time her cell service dropped in the middle of a call.

The men gathered around Griffin while Blue headed her way. She grabbed Tenny's hand and tugged. "Let's go. We need to put our bull-finding skills to use."

Rather than say *what bull finding skills*, she trotted beside Blue as they worked their way to the gate, which stood closed. Blue blew out a breath and released her grip on Tenny to scrub back the hair that sweat had plastered to her brow. "I think we should start here. When Griffin arrived, the unlatched gate stood open."

"No chance Rupert could have opened it?"

"I asked." She grimaced. "Turns out the gate had been sticking a little. Sometimes it wouldn't open, other times it wouldn't close. Usually, Griffin pulled it up hard, which made everything fall into place. As you probably know," Blue paused and pressed both hands to her heart, "the cows are our babies. We do a walk-by each night to make sure everyone is bedded down for the night. Rupert has his own box stall separate from the girls. Griffin puts him up last and lets him out first. Whatever happened to him occurred between six and ten a.m. when Griffin first texted me."

It was not a large time window—surely people would notice a

bull out on the road. She'd encountered enough livestock while driving, and the appropriate protocol consisted of stopping at the nearest farm and describing the animal in question. Some folks might try to bring the animal with them to show, but not Tenny. She tried to avoid wrangling animals, especially pigs, who could be slippery and mean. What she needed to do was get in the bull mindset. Rather than open the gate, she scrambled over the fence into the field. She let her head hang low and brought her closed fists up to her chest. A bull wouldn't have hands. She meandered to the gate in a slow bovine fashion and bumped it with her shoulder. It stayed closed. As a big bull, Rupert resembled a sumo wrestler more than a lightweight like her. Putting a little more muscle into it, she bumped the gate harder with her shoulder. "Ouch."

Blue bent her knees a little to make eye contact. "What are you doing, besides hurting yourself?"

"I'm trying to get into a bull mindset. Rupert's bored and trying to leave. So far, I've discovered if he happens to be a skinny librarian who can't use her hands, he's not getting out of this field."

"But he did," Blue pointed out. "Pretending to be a bull isn't exactly mystery-solving skills."

"Maybe not." Tenny put her hands on the gate, returning to a librarian while fighting an uncooperative latch. "This is hard to open."

Blue pushed up on the latch, and after a few seconds of wrestling and grunting, the gate swung open. Since it technically took four hands and knowledge of the sticky latch, Tenny doubted Rupert let himself out. Should she mention her suspicions and destroy all hope? If someone had taken Rupert, they couldn't use him for stud since his name made him valuable. Without his name and extensive pedigree, along with his various awards, he was just another bull. A thought occurred to her. "Is Rupert micro-chipped?"

"Like a dog?" Blue's eyes announced her confusion.

"Yeah, like a dog."

"I don't know. We never chipped the girls. They each have an ear tag for identification purposes. It helps us record milking output, health, breeding, and age. The tags are federally mandated. It helps track cows moved across state lines, which could be important if you have a bovine outbreak. Rupert has a big blue ear tag with a one on it, since he's the only bull."

Federally mandated. That changed things. Even though cows weren't dogs, she'd heard Blue brag on numerous occasions that her cows were purebred and better than the cows at surrounding farms. She naturally assumed her friend tended toward a natural bias when it came to the girls.

"Are they registered?"

"Most are. It's usually eighty dollars to register a cow. Not a huge amount when you consider the cost of a cow. We don't keep all the calves but we can easily sell the registered ones for a nice profit with Rupert being the sire. We like to keep the herd around sixty, since that is how much we can handle with the milking machines. Any more and we would need more than Cody helping us milk."

"Okay." Tenny cleared her throat. "We know Rupert has an ear tag that identifies him. He's also registered, which means no one could really show him or advertise him for stud. So..." She lengthened the word, having doubts about her theory. "...do you think he might be held for ransom?"

Blue regarded her as though she'd just bitten into an unripe persimmon, with narrowed eyes and a puckered mouth. Either the idea horrified her, knowing a photo with the sizable bull blindfolded and a ransom demand created from cut-out letters of uneven sizes might arrive, or then again, she may have found the possibility ridiculous.

Chapter Eleven

TENNY SQUATTED AND inspected the trampled grass, searching for a clue under the noonday sunlight while she waited for her best friend, Blue, to respond to her initial comment about Rupert's possible cow-napping. No obvious clues waited in bent grass, but it might depend on having actual tracking skills. All those nature shows had the host easily tracking an animal, using footprints, broken branches, trees they may have scratched on, leaving noticeable hair, and a flattened area where it had lain down to sleep. While bovines can catch a few winks on their feet, deep sleep occurred only when they rested their hooves.

Several emotions chased across Blue's face, but none stayed long enough to distinguish themselves. Finally, she choked out a loud laugh, and then another one. Talk about perplexing behavior. Tenny straightened to her full height and reached for her friend's arm. "Are you okay?"

Blue shook her head hard, stilling her laughter, and then inhaled hard, stifling a cry that showed signs of taking over.

"Ah, Blue." Tenny half-embraced her friend. "Forget I said anything."

"How can I?" Blue managed the words in a choked voice. "It makes no sense. Everyone knows we have no money. What could they expect to get by taking Rupert?"

Good question, but not one Tenny could answer. "Oh, honey." She patted her friend's back three times while stalling for something appropriate to say. Too bad Aunt Cinnamon couldn't tell her what to say. Not only did her aunt have pithy sayings to fit the occasion, but she also had stories of how people similar to Tenny overcame their own problems. At the time, Tenny depended on those tales for a dose of courage and optimism. It never occurred to that her aunt spun encouraging tales on the run. Maybe she could do likewise. "I'm sure Rupert just took a little walk. Maybe he was looking for clover or possibly had his eye on a cute Angus heifer."

Blue wiped her eyes and sniffed. "Rupert would never go for an Angus heifer. He's all Holstein, forever and ever."

While no expert on cattle, Tenny doubted a bull differentiated between breeds. "That is as it should be. We have to put on our thinking caps and figure out where he went."

"Thinking caps." Blue lifted her head and smirked. "Are you a hundred years old? You sound like our second-grade teacher, Miss Maisy."

A hundred years old. She doubted even Miss Maisy had reached her centennial birthday. She stepped back from her friend, almost certain Blue would find the inner strength to endure what would turn out to be a minor hiccup in her life. "Did anyone check the barn? How about the fields with all the girls, which seems like the most natural place for him to be, especially since he was supposed to be meeting up with his girlfriends today?"

"I don't know." Blue pulled out her phone and pecked at the keyboard, picking out letters one at a time—an excruciatingly slow process. Tenny cleared her throat.

"Who are you texting?"

"Griffin, my husband."

"I know who Griffin is." Tenny looked over her shoulder to where Griffin stood with a gaggle of gesturing men who had probably come up with a half-dozen different ways they should search for Rupert. "You know, he's just over there. You could walk over and ask him, which would be a whole lot quicker than your hunt-and-peck texting."

"Shush. You're not so fast yourself."

"It's all the autocorrect my phone keeps doing."

"Sure it is. Besides, what if my dear, sweet husband didn't look in the barn or the field? If I mention this in front of the other men, he'd look silly. They also would never let him forget it and come up with some weird nickname like The Bull Loser."

"Not the cleverest nickname, but it could happen. Maybe we should check out the barn and field ourselves. If we find Rupert, you could just text Griffin something like *come home*."

"You're right." She held up her phone. "I haven't even success-fully typed Rupert. Stupid autocorrect changed it to running, ruptured, rupees, and ruler, as if I don't know what I'm saying. I'll go get the truck."

Energized with a purpose, Blue's short legs took extra-long steps, making her look like a pony trying to keep pace with a horse. Maybe she should have walked with her. Was Blue going to drive the truck up to the gate? The lack of rain had already done a number on the grass. Bare patches dotted the area both inside and outside the fence. The iconic light bulb flashed over her head as she patted her front pants pocket to locate her phone. She worked her way over to the first bare spot, keeping to the grass, and bent down to stare. Some bird tracks and a dying weed—neither equating to a smoking gun.

Aware Blue may have reached the truck, Tenny moved to the next bare spot. This one had a single tire tread—a directional pattern, not unusually large or small, but an average size suiting almost any vehicle except the mega truck with four wheels in the back for hauling. It could be Griffin's vehicle, or even Blue's, or one of the various people who'd been in the field these past few drought-stricken weeks. Would the impression get blown away or stay in the flaky soil? Kneeling, she reached to touch the imprint but pulled her hand away before doing so. First things first. She took out her cell and snapped a photo. Who knows? Maybe she could compare it to the various vehicles around town—showing up at folk's houses and farms to examine their tires didn't serve as a working plan. Her fingers dusted across the dirt near the imprint. Soft dirt easily smashed under her fingers, which made the imprint recent.

A horn honk reminded her that Blue never liked waiting. Tenny pocketed her cell with its precious picture and sprinted across the field the best she could without resembling a red-headed giraffe running. This was a term Rita had coined in primary school and used it whenever they had recess. Thank goodness the name Tenny stuck as opposed to Red Giraffe. Gasping a little, she opened the truck's door and hauled herself into the cab. "Where's a place I can check out everyone's vehicle?"

Blue crossed her arms and sniffed. "You aren't planning on egging Rita's car?"

"No."

"Too bad. I would have covered for you. I imagine everyone will be at the fair come Thursday. We expect to be there, too."

There was no need to add that they expected to show their cows.

Even though the fair existed for the young 4-H kids who raised a calf, created a wooden box, or made muffins as a project to show off their skills, the local dairies had a presence, too, as did the various horse clubs. Many adults competed against one another for bragging rights and a purple roseate ribbon. Both her aunt and uncle had participated every year. In the small town of Emerson, the fair served as the event of the year.

"No worries," she reassured her friend as she crossed her fingers. "I won't engage in egg throwing. I bet Rupert will be back by then."

Chapter Twelve

INSTEAD OF USING the road as almost anyone else would do, Blue steered the truck across the bumpy field and up to the red and white barns. The biggest one featured a smiling cow announcing *Milk Makes a Body Happy, Moo Town Dairy* in six-foot letters arched above the cow spokes-animal. One huge pothole made the truck suspension whine along with Tenny. "What's wrong with using the road?"

"I'm saving my husband from being labeled foolish when I find Rupert still in his box stall. Maybe he only *thought* he let him out."

"Ah yeah." No cheerful sayings came to mind that involved a man missing an almost two-thousand-pound bull. Lacking her aunt's store of positive anecdotes, she settled for the one thing she knew to do when a subject became sticky—change it. "You think Rita is trying to get Dallas back?"

"Absolutely! If only to make a big public scene where she kicks him to the curb. Despite all the damage control, news leaked out that he filed first." Blue's lips twisted with the pronouncement, expressing her opinion on the matter. "That's the problem when you only have one lawyer in town and his wife, Philomena, the receptionist, gossips. There may be some oath lawyers take about not revealing confidential client information. Unfortunately, Philomena never took it."

Even though she only wanted to change the conversation, Tenny found herself sucked into her own conversational change. Hating herself for asking, she did anyhow. "How might Rita win Dallas back?"

The truck tires grabbed onto the driveway blacktop with a jerk as Blue steered toward the farthest barn. "Hmm." She hummed the word and then snorted. "Not the way any ordinary woman might do. Yeah, most women might invite their ex over for a gourmet supper, write a long apology note, or even gift him with tickets to a sporting event or favorite band concert tickets. Rita doesn't cook. She would never take responsibility for anything, which would make it hard to say 'I'm sorry.' I'm sure she has no clue about anything Dallas likes. More likely, she'll just keep putting her fabulous self right in front of Dallas, assuming he'll fall on his knees and beg her to come back."

"Do you think it'll work?"

"Nope." Blue put the truck in park and switched off the ignition. She swung open the door and shimmied across the seat, ready to vault out of the vehicle, and added, "It might work on most of the guys in Emerson." Her nose crinkled. "Amazing what bad treatment they'd accept, just to be seen with the high-maintenance princess. Not Dallas, though. If she knows him, she'll know that he's the kind of guy who wants to help. Kind of a knight in armor swooping in on the scene to rescue the damsel, stranded motorist, or lost pet." She forced a small chuckle. "In our case, it's a misplaced bull. Let's hope Rita doesn't resort to any of those little-ol'-me-needs-a-certain-man-to-rescue-me ploys."

Tenny blew out an audible breath as she opened her door and

slid out. It was an irritating possibility. Good Knight Dallas might already be embroiled in a rescue mission. She fell in step with Blue as they entered the barn. Her friend curved her hands around her mouth and yelled, "Rupert!"

A half-grown feral tiger-striped kitten sauntering across the straw-strewn barn floor stopped, took fright, jumped up in the air, and when he landed, scampered behind the feed barrels. No moos sounded, and no cows turned in their general direction. The sunlight streamed through the open doors and windows, highlighting the dust motes in the air. Nothing here. Well, make that no bull, but there were plenty of stacks of hay, feed barrels, and boxes haphazardly stacked against one wall. Despite the obvious absence of Rupert, Blue peered into each empty stall as if the large animal might be hiding, flattened against the ground.

The opportunistic flies buzzed as they surveyed the barn on a quest for their next meal. A heavy sigh escaped Blue, and she leaned heavily against a large box stall, which probably served as Rupert's. It stood away from the others, a trio of small rooms separating it. Tenny moved to stand beside her friend, resting her arms in the open door. "Rupert's?"

"Yeah," Blue replied with weariness and defeat soaking the word. She pointed to the rooms. "Many people don't keep a bull in the same barn with the cows. At first, we didn't. We made this mini barn away from the rest of the buildings, but it was such a hassle going back and forth. Griffin wasn't comfortable with his expensive bull being so far away from the house. I used to tease him and say he loved Rupert more than me." She sniffed and wiped away a tear with her hand. "Anyhow," she paused to clear her throat, "when he discovered Rupert wasn't a beast like some of those out-of-control bulls, he suggested building a series of offices to block Rupert's view and smell of the gals. We did that. Eventually, Griffin relaxed enough to build the little shed in the field for Rupert. Oddly, the guy likes his moonlight pasture time." Her hands tightened on the rail she grasped. "All the same, we put him up last night."

"I know you did." Even though she said the words, Tenny had no clue what happened to the cows the night before. She knew Griffin and Blue treated their cows like beloved children. If they said they tucked them all into their stalls with a goodnight kiss and a lullaby, she believed it. All the same, sixty-plus cows spread across three barns must be a huge undertaking to put away every night.

Blue twisted around with a spark in her eyes. "We're not done by far. Let's go check the south pasture where the girls are grazing."

While Tenny understood the words *pasture* and *south*, they meant nothing to her when strung together. "Are we walking to the pasture or driving?"

"Walking." Blue placed a hand on her hip and angled her head. "No worries. The gals can't be more than half a mile away. We only have so much land. I may have been tearing all over the place in the truck, but I'd never drive over prime pasture land. Besides, we put a lot of work into seeding pastures with Kentucky bluegrass and Tall Fescue. It makes for better milk. Griffin has tried his hand at buffel and Mitchell grass." She shrugged. "They're popular in Australia, but have had issues taking root here. Maybe in time."

The two of them left the barn together and headed in a southern direction. Another truck waited beside Blue's and the sun silhouetted Griffin, who removed his hat and waved it at them. Naturally, they changed their direction and rambled up to him.

"Hey, honey," Blue said and kissed him on the cheek. "Can I get you anything?"

He wrapped one arm around her and gave her a tight half-embrace. "You could do me a favor."

"Anything. Name it." Her brow furrowed as she gazed at her husband.

He gave her nose an affectionate tap. "That's what I love about you. Always so ready to help." Griffin paused, tensed, and then said, "I need you to stop looking for Rupert."

Blue blinked a few times and practically shouted, "What?"

"Trust me, sweetheart. It's for the best. I have this covered." He dropped his arm, shoved his hat back on his head and nodded in Tenny's direction. "You need to get your friend home. I'm sure she has a lot to do with settling the estate and starting her bookmobile business." He gentled the statement with a slight smile. "Along with fending off all her potential beaus."

Tenny's open hand went up as if to halt his suggestion. She grimaced. "It's more likely I fend off the hopeful mamas." Knowing when she'd been shown the figurative door, she said, "See ya, and good luck."

Griffin said goodbye and headed to the house. As the two women walked to the truck together, Blue grumbled, "Did you see what he did there? He tricked me. Used my love for him to have me agreeing to something I normally wouldn't have agreed to."

"Tricky," she felt obliged to say. "Weird. I know Griffin, and he isn't one of those high-handed fellows who barks out commands to his wife."

"So not."

"That makes me wonder why he would do such a thing now. When has he ever forbade you to do anything?"

The question stopped Blue in her tracks, her eyes rolled upward as she pondered the possibility. "Not ever, really." She held up one finger. "Wait! I once fell off the ladder leading to the hay loft and twisted my ankle. After that, he told me I couldn't go up in the hayloft because he didn't want to take a chance on me getting hurt. It was just a stupid accident. While on the ladder, I thought I heard something fall, and I twisted a little to see what it was. Since I had clogs on, which are probably not recommended for ladder climbing, I lost my balance. Somehow, I can't convince him that I won't tumble off the ladder again."

"All right. What I hear is Griffin won't let you do anything he thinks is dangerous for you."

Blue's lips twisted a little, and she crinkled her nose before replying. "Put that way, it sounds more about love than his turning into a dictator overnight."

"True. It also means whatever he thinks happened to Rupert could be troublesome, and he doesn't want you involved."

Blue stomped her booted foot. "He may have hogtied me, but he hasn't outsmarted me."

"How's that?"

"He didn't tell *you* that you couldn't look for Rupert."

It was not hard to see the convoluted path Blue's mind created. "If I choose to look for your bull, how would I relate any info to you, especially since you're not supposed to look for it?"

"Please. We have a bookmobile business to handle." With that, she gave a hard wink and headed for the truck with a bounce in her step. Tenny watched for a few steps before hurrying to catch up with her. Even though she often called her aunt Cinnamon a force of nature, she might have to add Blue to the list, too.

Chapter Thirteen

THERE WAS NO need to ask Blue's opinion on her husband's latest directive. Nope. No need to ask at all because she carried on a running monologue about Griffin acting like a pig-headed caveman. She added that if he thought she'd sit still for such behavior, he had another thing coming. By this point, all Tenny's sympathy moved more toward Griffin—the man would need it.

When Blue pulled up in front of the house, Tenny reached over and patted her friend's arm. "Would you like to come inside? Have a snack or something? You know I have plenty of goodies."

Despite their adventures, a couple of hours of afternoon remained, along with a full evening—hours she'd spend alone. Normally, she'd entertain herself when left alone. She even considered herself lucky to move into an apartment on her own, as opposed to sharing a unit and all the problems that came with roommates.

Back then, she knew what to do. Everything from polishing off the latest mystery novel to creating dioramas. Her diorama passion burst full-blown when a fourth-grade project called for a scene from a favorite book. Most kids glued green army men into shoe boxes even if their book was *Little Women*. Not Tenny. With the help of Uncle Mark, she had created a small farm for the *Little House on the*

Prairie family and dressed each tiny person in period-appropriate clothing she'd sewn. The project earned her an A and much praise. It was a red-letter day for her since she'd never considered herself good at anything. Her friend's silence made her question if she'd somehow missed her answer, lost in remembering a more pleasant time.

Blue stared straight ahead, squinting a little but not speaking. Finally, she pointed at the living room double windows. "Were those screens always torn?"

Her head whipped around so fast that her neck cracked. Tenny glared through her glasses. A little smudgy from their day, she pulled them off and rubbed them on a clean spot on her shirt and shoved them back onto her face. A ragged tear along the bottom of the frames left the rest of the screen flapping in the wind. Flies and mosquitoes had now received a personal invitation to come inside. By the metal glider, shards and dirt from a cracked pot littered the porch floor, along with a dying geranium. A rumbling started low as her hands clenched and she clamped her molars together. Cinnamon sometimes teased Tenny about having the perfect personality to be a librarian. Besides her love of reading, she never raised her voice—except for very rare occasions.

"Precious!" She growled the name as her eyes surveyed the front yard, looking for the masked culprit who had the good sense to flee the crime scene.

Blue clicked her tongue and added, "Even though he probably has a brain the size of a pea, he probably didn't stick around to get your opinion on his handiwork. Besides, you can't get upset with him for being what he is."

Really? After Blue gave her the lecture about keeping him out of the house, now she's defending him? "I can't believe you're on his side! I won't be able to have the windows open tonight."

"Not *those* windows. There are other windows—unless he tore out those screens, too."

Tenny moaned. Why did everything have to be so hard? Her hands tented over her nose and mouth as she held in the sob. Trying to remember the instructions on keeping calm that the university doctor told incoming freshmen, she sucked in a deep breath, mentally counting to four, and then let it out slowly, counting to five. Her hands trembled and heat still wafted off her face, evidence that calm eluded her. Irritated, she sniffed, dropped her hands, and grumbled, "Not sure why you're so happy."

"Not happy," Blue clarified with a nod. "Satisfied that I was right. I did warn you about that overgrown rodent."

"You did," Tenny admitted with a frown. "Raccoons aren't rodents. They belong to the Procyonidae family. They are more closely related to olingos and coatis."

"Thank you, Reference Librarian. I'll assume whatever you just mentioned are equally annoying critters in other countries."

"Basically."

"Precious will always be a rodent to me. Tearing up stuff, gobbling your food..." Her nose crinkled as she continued, "...And leaving nasty calling cards each visit."

"Calling cards?" Tenny's brow furrowed as she imagined Precious presenting a calling card with cursive writing announcing *Precious, Esquire*. A tiny raccoon print might grace the card, too. She blinked when she comprehended what Blue meant by the term. "Aunt Cinnamon trained him. He goes outside. He only comes inside for meals."

"Or when he can break in," Blue reminded.

Tenny held up her hand, not wanting to hear a recital of all the bad things Precious could do. There was a good chance she'd experience them on her own. "I'm going." She suited her actions to her words and opened her door. "I appreciate your taking me out to see the bus. Even if it didn't work out."

"Yeah." Blue packed the word with all the disappointment of the day. "You know..." She forced cheer into her voice, but it came off sounding fake, rather like those dolls who talk when you squeeze their hand and say *I love you* in a stilted manner. "...there are probably half a dozen buses for sale in the area."

"That many?" The number surprised her. She'd already swung her feet around to slide out but inquired as she did so, "Why would someone buy a school bus only to sell it again? Do we have a lot of dissatisfied school bus drivers?"

"I imagine we do. Mainly, folks want to jump on the skoolie wagon and convert a school bus they got for cheap into a luxury camper or a tiny home. Then they discover how much the conversion will cost and all the hours of work involved. Suddenly, it doesn't seem like such a great plan."

"Not your best pep talk." Tenny's feet hit the ground, and she held the truck door open as she addressed her friend.

"Oh no! Not you. I didn't mean you. It can't be *that* much work making a bus into a bookmobile. Slap together a few shelves. Possibly carpet it for sound absorption. Tack up some READ posters and you're good to go."

"Well, it might take more than that." She paused, trying to consider what might be involved. "I need to research this and find out if there are any regulations. Surely someone has posted an article or two online." She shut the door, waved, and turned to go up her sidewalk and discover what damage Precious had wreaked upon the house.

The buzz of the electric window going down had Tenny turning. Blue leaned out of the truck and yelled, "Make sure to contact the lawyer and find out just how much money you have to spend!"

The closest neighbor, who'd been quietly deadheading her flowers when they arrived, glanced up. Even two middle school girls on bikes slowed down as if to listen. The art of eavesdropping started young, but anything shouted outside shouldn't count as snooping. Tenny held a finger to her lips. No doubt she'd be called a money-grubbing city girl in ten minutes or less on the gossip hotline—never mind that she grew up in Emerson.

Blue grimaced and stuck out her thumb and pinky to indicate a phone and held it up to her ear. Yeah, she'd call her bestie later, maybe much later, depending on the damage Precious did. Tenny returned the phone gesture, and then waved before she trudged to the front door, managing to ignore any nosy neighbors hoping to talk. Past tired, a self-made spa day might serve with a face mask and soaking neck-deep in bubbles with cucumber slices on her eyes.

Chapter Fourteen

THE AIR HUNG silent and humid inside the house. Pulled curtains and closed blinds dimmed the afternoon sun but contributed to a general lethargic atmosphere—like napping or not quite able to shake off a stupor. Tenny closed the door and waited, expecting for the briefest moment for a welcome called out from the kitchen. When no one spoke, she shook her head. How could she keep forgetting? For all practical purposes, her family no longer existed. Willow, her birth mother, could be kicking around somewhere. She might have even had another child, giving Tenny a half-sibling. Finding it hard to know how to handle such a possibility, Tenny defaulted to her tried and true way of managing difficult things—not thinking about it. It kept close company with her other coping mechanism—changing the subject.

Her shod feet padded across the living room rug, creating the only noise. Her nose twitched when she entered the kitchen. Aunt Cinnamon taught her to recognize spices by smell alone. It was not exactly the equivalent of winning the spelling bee or a grand championship ribbon, but her aunt took pride in her ability, often asking her to name ingredients in a finished dish just by inhaling the aroma. Occasionally, she even had Tenny demonstrate her skill. Most locals valued Cinnamon's friendship and excellent cooking, so they feigned astonishment. A slow inhale informed her that the sweets on the table had lost their freshness. Their closeness to each other caused their aromas to blend, dulling the appetizing factor. That was no surprise with the heat and loose coverings, which meant she'd end up dumping a few.

She peeled up the foil on the pineapple upside-down cake—a personal favorite—and deemed it save-worthy. The cake Precious had ravaged automatically ended up in the toss pile. After going through about six of the delectable goodies, Tenny sighed. "It's too hot for this."

Uncertain about the state of the screens, she settled for turning on the box fans set about the house, which created a low hum and a breeze. On muggy days like these, her aunt used to prepare her an ice bath. A single ice cube might be added to the cool water along with a couple of drops of mint oil or freshly picked leaves. She closed her eyes, trying to hold on to the memory. "Ice bath. That's what I need."

Opening her eyes, she slipped out the back door in search of fresh mint leaves. There was a good chance there might be an email inquiry about returning to her old job or filling in for a pregnancy leave. Right now, relaxing in a cool tub with a freshly made face mask and possibly listening to music served as her total plan. Maybe later, she'd do something a bit more constructive and tackle whatever showed up in her inbox. Excited about her homemade spa treatment, she tore leaves from a lush mint plant near the back steps and darted back into the house, certain Precious would follow her if in the area. After her bath, she'd have a look for the raccoon.

The water pressure had never been great and made filling the tub a project. Tenny rubbed the mint leaves on the tub interior and then turned on the water. In the kitchen, she consulted her phone for homemade facial masks but discovered most required ingredients leaning toward the exotic side and were not accessible in the kitchen, or Emerson for that matter. She settled on one with lemon, honey, turmeric, and banana, which was guaranteed to make her skin glow. In between checking on the bath water level, she smashed the ingredients into a yellowy paste.

Grabbing her uncle Mark's radio on the way to the bathroom, she plugged it in once she reached her destination and searched for something soothing on the dial. Snippets of country music, farm reports, and angry talk radio seeped out as she twisted the knob. So not what she wanted. Inside the cassette tape portion of the radio, a tape rested. Curious, Tenny pulled it out and read the title. "Simon & Garfunkel. *Bridge Over Troubled Water.*" She snorted. "Sounds about right." She replaced the tape and pushed *play*. A melodic voice sang about feeling weary, small, and in tears. She almost decided against listening to it, but she remembered her uncle's raspy baritone belting out the words.

Her aunt's bright floral shower cap covered her hair as she applied the honey-scented goo to her face. Carefully, she undressed, trying not to get any of the facial mixture on her clothes. Any rational person would have undressed first, and normally, she would have. Blaming it on exhaustion, both mental and physical, she slipped into the bath water with a sigh and a splash. Her current concerns drifted away with the music. Her eyes closed as she tried to recall something her uncle had said about the bridge song.

Bridge over troubled waters referred to someone going through hard times. For all intents and purposes, no one could be found to help them. "Could be me." She reached for a pouf and lathered it up with vanilla bath gel. "That's self-pity talking." She could have sworn the voice belonged to her aunt, but she recognized it as her own. Whenever her aunt's stories, tailored for the situation, failed to work their magic, she'd remind Tenny to count her blessings. If Tenny failed to come up with any, Cinnamon did, naming a loving family, a safe home, food to eat, clothes to wear—the list could go on indefinitely. "I do have a home, food to eat, and friends."

A loud knock on the front door carried all the way through the house. "Ah, speaking of friends." Tenny waited to see if the knock would come again. A strolling solicitor wouldn't wait around long. However, a salesperson must be desperate to drive this far out to peddle their product. She couldn't remember anyone going door to door, except for Girl Scouts, and it wasn't cookie season. Another knock sounded. It *could* be Blue.

Why wouldn't she have called instead? A quick survey around the bathroom revealed no phone. Maybe she *had* called and when Tenny didn't answer, she drove over, certain something had happened. With a groan, she stood, stepped out of the tub, and wrapped herself in Uncle Mark's ratty plaid robe. After his death, her aunt wore it instead of her own frilly lavender one. She claimed it helped her to feel close to her late husband. As for Tenny, she just didn't have any clean clothes.

She'd reassure Blue and then finish her bath. Barefooted, she marched across the floor, her wet feet slapping the wooden surface. At the door, Tenny swung it open, talking as she did so. "See! I'm still alive."

"Tenny?" Dallas queried as if unsure of her identity. One hand shot through his hair. "You're looking a little jaundiced."

"What?" His comment confused her as she scratched her chin

and came back with gooey fingers. "Oh no!" Her stomach somersaulted as she flushed hard under her banana turmeric mask. "Facial mask. Trying to relax with a bath." Her first impulse was to slam the door, but he'd seen her and she'd confirmed her identity, too. What else could happen? She forced a laugh. "You know women. Always trying to improve on what nature gave us. I imagine you saw Rita with plenty of beauty products slathered across her face."

"Actually, no," he confessed, shoving his hands into his jean pockets.

Seriously? He must be lying about it. Tenny sniffed. "Of course not. I'm sure she never had to embellish her natural beauty."

As soon as she said the words, she wanted to retrieve the petty comment. At the corner of the porch stairs, she witnessed the tip of a dark tail sliding away. She leaned to her right, trying to see around Dallas. It could be a cat, but it was probably Precious, hoping to slip in unnoticed—totally what she didn't need. Her eyes shifted from side to side, trying to pick out a familiar masked face among the flower pots and porch furniture.

"Oh, Rita would never be caught with a face mask on at home. Everything she did had to be done by a professional in an expensive salon with a fancy foreign name most people couldn't pronounce. I wouldn't have minded a home facial. Something about it would have made her more real."

A pair of lively eyes peeked out from under the turquoise porch chair, resulting in Tenny's slamming the door. "Aha!" She breathed the words with a sense of triumph and then realized she had slammed the door on Dallas while he rambled on about Rita. Well, maybe he deserved it. No local girl wanted to hear the glories of Rita, having heard them numerous times, mostly *from* Rita. Hadn't he said something about how he wished she used a home face mask because it made her down to earth or something?

Aunt Cinnamon would have been horrified at her rude behavior. She cracked the door a few inches, searching for any sign of her nemesis. None. "Sorry. I thought I saw Precious."

"Oh really?" Dallas turned full circle, cocking his head one way, then another. He probably thought she just made it up to explain the door's slamming. Of course there would be no critter when she needed him to appear. "I don't see him anywhere."

"He's tricky." There was not much else she could say. Festus, Uncle Mark's friend and self-proclaimed comic, strolled by and waved, and then stopped, did a double take and shouted, "I didn't know it was Halloween already!"

"Ha ha!" She played along. "I'm getting a head start."

Festus laughed, pointed at Dallas, and asked, "You going as a zombie, too?"

"Possibly." Dallas graciously turned to address the man. "There's always being a dead farmer," he teased. "I can just add a little catsup to my regular clothes."

The hearty laughter carried as Festus slapped his leg, so taken with the quip. He finally straightened, saluted Dallas, and continued walking.

Afraid she might have to exchange words with another neighbor still smeared with her facial mix, she gripped the door with both hands and explained, "I need to get this off my face before it hardens. Why did you come by?"

"Ah, that." He shuffled his feet and then made eye contact. "The county fair is starting, and it's our one big event. I was wondering..." He paused and cleared his throat. "...if you weren't doing anything, if you'd like to go to the fair with me. You could pick the night. As you probably remember, there's the hot dog eating contest, the talent show, the sheepdog herding contest, and the truck pull. You can decide."

Did she hear him right? She blinked, grabbed a healthy bit of skin on her left arm, and pinched. That hurt! Which meant she probably wasn't asleep in the tub.

Dallas sucked in his lips, released them, and then continued speaking. "If you don't want to go, I understand."

"Oh, no, I *do* want to go." The reality of her secret teenage fantasy taking form rattled her even more than looking like a jaundiced zombie. Keeping her eyes open, she counted to five mentally before screaming "Yes!" like a demented fool. A slow deep breath calmed her racing heart, and she employed her subdued reference librarian voice. "Sheepdog herding contest. You'll have to tell me what night that is." She stretched her face into a wide grin but could feel her skin tightening. "I'll talk to you later. I have to go scrub my face back to its normal color."

"See you. I'll call," Dallas promised as she closed the door. Overwhelmed that her school heartthrob had asked her out, she leaned against the door in a romantic haze. When her vision cleared, she noticed a certain raccoon sitting upright on the couch as if he were a person.

"Precious." She whispered the name, but for once she chose not to chase him.

Chapter Fifteen

HER FACE SCRUBBED clean, dressed in shorts and another book tee, Tenny picked up a frying pan, holding it like a microphone, and sang, "You're the falling star!" her voice cracking on the last word as she danced around her kitchen. The late afternoon sun spotlighted her as it streamed through the sunroom windows. The windows on three sides made the room both sunny and hot and a bit like Florida. Her nose crinkled at the sour note, and she stuck out her tongue. Tenny pointed directly at her guest. "Let me hear you do better."

Instead of breaking into song, Precious' beady eyes regarded her solemnly, and he broke into incomprehensible chatter. When done, he pulled out a peach tea bottle he must have been hiding behind his back and twisted off the lid before lifting it with both hands to his mouth.

His action pricked a tiny hole in Tenny's balloon of happiness created by the unexpected date with Dallas. It wasn't enough to truly upset her, but enough to cause a brief frown as she used the frying pan as an extension of her arm while pointing at her masked visitor. "You'd better remember we're in a truce. Doing things like dipping into my Peach Snapple Tea supply will end it? *Capische?*"

Precious took another swig of the tea, demonstrating that he neither understood nor cared. His actions pulled a sigh from the current homeowner. All the same, Tenny placed the pan on the stove and then pulled out eggs, milk, and butter.

"Don't get used to my fixing you a meal. You're a wild animal, after all. You should be outside eating nuts and berries. Insects, crayfish, and the occasional frog might figure into your diet. Any eggs you consume would be raw. I'm only doing this because of your grieving Aunt Cinnamon." She gave a small sniff and glanced back at the animal, certain his eyes grew glassy at the mention of his former benefactor.

His silence could have served as agreement or disagreement. Tenny believed Precious understood and totally supported her plan to wean him off regular homemade meals. First, she'd have to quit making them. For now, she appreciated the company. His tiny claw-tipped left hand reached toward a foil-wrapped pan while maintaining eye contact—amazingly sneaky. Out in the real world, he'd be a pickpocket—his only issue would be that a raccoon in the city would stick out.

"Stop that! I see what you're doing." She seized the aluminum pie pan in question, pulling it out of reach. A peek under the foil revealed Old Man Titus' famous apple pie. Normally, Tenny considered herself quite the fan of apple pies, but not Titus'. The elderly man showed up at events with something he'd baked—usually a fruit pie that included one sizable onion. Unlike dessert recipes that called for tomato soup, making the product creamier or richer with no hint of tomato, you could definitely taste the onion in Titus' pies. It overpowered the fruit. He often bragged he used his mother's recipe. Cinnamon explained that when people lacked ingredients, they made substitutions. Apparently, Titus' family grew onions by the bushels, which meant they served as the missing ingredient. People choked down small slivers of his pies at church suppers and pitch-in dinners, never letting on how they truly felt. Fortunately, he never made *big* pies.

She might as well let Precious have a slice—it might cure his desire to eat human food. Then again, it might go down better than days-old garbage. She cut a small triangle and placed it in a ceramic dish she'd unearthed from under the sink. In her aunt's familiar scrawl, *Precious* stood out against the white bowl. The raccoon abandoned his drink, jumped off the chair, and scampered to the food dish.

Curious, Tenny waited with one hand on her hip, humming the song she'd been singing earlier. Using his surprisingly primate-like hands, he broke off a piece and dipped it in the water dish before placing it in his mouth. Instead of chewing or swallowing, he landed an intense glare on Tenny and spit out the morsel onto the floor.

"That's all on you, buddy. You wanted a sample. I was kind of hoping you'd love it and polish it off. I know Titus will ask me if I ate it. This way I could say the pan was scraped clean and enjoyed immensely without any mention of who'd consumed it. I should have suspected you'd been spoiled with Cinnamon's cooking."

The raccoon balanced on his two hind legs, waving his front legs, trying to make a point, but he looked more like a conductor trying to justify his high salary by waving at the various orchestra sections as if they didn't know the song. "Okay," Tenny agreed. "It was mean of me to serve you onion pie. All the same, you could have eaten it. *I* have on numerous occasions."

She opened a cabinet and pulled out a mixing bowl at the same time as her phone rang. Thinking it might be Dallas since he had mentioned calling, she scooped up the phone and answered it before even looking at the caller ID. She gasped. "Hello?"

"That was fast," Blue remarked from the other end. "Most of the time it rings four or five times and often, I get voice mail. Did you have the phone in your hand?"

"Close." Unwilling to admit that she thought it was Dallas, she went to the obvious reason for Blue to call. "Did you find Rupert?"

"Not really, but we have a good idea where he is."

Blue's weary voice held a touch of amusement that baffled Tenny. "Explain."

"Remember Kevin Slaughter from school?"

Her eyebrows went up and her teeth clenched. She remembered him all too well. "The practical joker who wrote messages on the toilet paper such as, *What's that smell?* and, *What have you been eating?* and then rerolled the tissue and put them in the girls' restroom at school."

Blue chuckled. "That's Kevin. He put the messaged TP in the boys' and the faculty restrooms, too."

"Doesn't make me feel any better." Her brow furrowed as she tried to decide how Kevin figured into the missing bull scenario. "Should I assume he's gotten any better as far as being a trickster?"

"That *depends* on what you mean."

Tenny noticed the emphasis on the word. "He quit playing jokes on people."

"Not exactly. His jokes evolved into more elaborate pranks that sometimes stretched into weeks. Once, he told us he was ordering a mail-order bride. Told everyone her name and what date she'd arrive. Almost everyone came together, making a special banner for Yulia and a barbeque dinner down at the park to welcome her."

"Let me guess. No Yulia?"

"Yulia turned out to be this white donkey who wandered into town when the bride was expected. Kevin claimed he'd been tricked. Maybe he did that so everyone wouldn't be mad at him, but Griffin knew it was a gag all along. They've been friends ever since their mamas laid their baby blankets next to each other at the Fourth of July festivities. Anyhow, after Griffin talked to the majority of the guys, they pointed the finger at Kevin. It sounded like something he'd do. The only problem is when you react in a negative fashion to one of his pranks, he considers it a challenge and comes up with a worse one."

Tenny snorted. "It's no wonder he's single."

"Yep. He had a few dates, but the rumor is they didn't end well, since he pranked his date in one way or another. Added salt to one of his date's coffee and served soy chicken nuggets to a vegetarian. You remember Wellsy? She's a vegetarian now."

"Ok. Understandable being brought up on a chicken farm." She thrust one hand through her hair and kept an eye on Precious, who had moved closer to the table of goodies. "Why so upset about soy chicken nuggets?"

"They weren't soy. He waited until she ate them to inform her otherwise."

"Ooh." Tenny winced, imagining an angry Wellsy. "Not cool. If Kevin has Rupert, how's Griffin going to handle it?"

Blue giggled and cleared her throat. "He's going to prank Kevin back by stealing Rupert back and hiding him, making Kevin think he's actually lost a valuable bull. Let him sweat it out. Griffin and friends are planning to dress in all black and check out the farm before committing the heist."

Tenny swiveled slightly, facing the living room as she spoke. One hand went up to rub her neck. "Listen to you. Griffin and his buds must think they're in an *Ocean's 11* movie or something."

Blue sniffed. "Only if, instead of money, they were trying to move a very large bull under the cover of night with no one the wiser."

"Good luck with that."

A metal pan thumped on the floor, followed by the crack of an egg. Tenny spun in time to see Precious mounted on the counter next to the stove with one egg in his hands. "Got to go. I have my own four-legged Kevin to handle."

Chapter Sixteen

A MOCKINGBIRD PERCHED right outside Tenny's bedroom window, demonstrating his repertoire of various avian songs, which were many. The concert lasted about forty-five minutes. While spot-on in his rendition of the calls, he usually started at four forty-five before dawn even pinked the sky. The moment of silence pulled a sigh of relief from Tenny as she rolled over, trying to find the perfect arrangement of limbs enabling her to fall back asleep. A little hazy around the edges, she drifted into a half-dreaming, half-musing state where she held hands with Dallas as they maneuvered around the long lines surrounding both the funnel cake stand and the corn dog vendor. Colorful bunting tied to game booths and the ticket stand fluttered in the wind. Dallas turned soft eyes on her and opened his mouth to speak, but only the sound of a blue jay shriek issued forth.

Her eyes popped open as she levitated an inch off the mattress. The screech of a barn owl came next, swiftly followed by the high-pitched whistle of a cedar waxwing. *Geesh.* She pushed up into a sitting position, glaring at the window as if the bird could sense her disapproval. As a well-read librarian, she knew the mockingbird, while noisy, wasn't the loudest bird in the area. The Great Horned Owl could be heard from over two miles away. No owls sat outside her window, thank goodness. Her own feathered troubadour moved onto its birds of prey repertoire.

"Might as well get up. Plenty to do."

Tenny stumbled through her morning routine while dreaming of coffee. A furry face pressed to the window glass startled her, causing Tenny to bump into a cabinet. She muttered under her breath, "Precious." The raccoon's expression hinted at being upset. He was possibly mad at Tenny for forcing him to sleep outside like an animal. Honestly, she couldn't ever remember Cinnamon allowing the critter to stay inside at night. Being a nocturnal creature, she could only imagine the mayhem he'd cause while she dozed.

"Good morning to you!" she sang out, trying to cover her initial fright. Pouring water into the drip coffee maker, she weighed letting Precious in or making him wait. What was the worst that could happen? Precious could get mad and go hang out in the woods with his kin. Her eyebrows lifted a little until a tiny raccoon hand hammered on the glass, causing it to shake. Uncle Mark told her the glass in the house was original. He acted as if that made it special. Cinnamon declared the glass to be drafty and wavy. All the same, she had no plans for replacing it. "Pest."

Today, she'd have to sit down and pay the bills. There was no need to add glass repair to the budget, especially since she had screens to replace. Wait a minute! Tenny peered at the window, complete with a raccoon face and no screen. She stomped one foot and shook her finger at Precious. "For that, I refuse to make you breakfast. I remember Aunt Cinnamon feeding you cat food when she got too busy for your favorite meals." Grim-faced, Tenny bent and searched under the sink for the bag of cat food. Once located, she poured some into a plastic mixing bowl, placed it on the outside step, and then slammed the door as Precious sprinted around the corner.

"I'm in no mood to deal with you."

Her cranky, sleep-deprived breakfast turned out to be the best time of her day. Who knew? If she had, Tenny might have lingered over her coffee or chewed her oatmeal more slowly. There were only so many times a person could chew oatmeal. Next on her list of things she needed to do, but had put off as long as possible, was to pay the bills. Tenny eyed the ever-growing stack of mail. Most of them were bills, she could feel it. Pastel envelopes addressed in spidery handwriting contained sympathy cards. Plain envelopes, often with no name on the return address, turned out to be some direct mail campaign for politicians, questionable organizations with religious names, or various diseases. The bills announced what they were on the outside. No need to play coy. Besides, who'd want to steal a bill?

Tenny dropped the checkbook, stamps, and return labels with her aunt's name on them on a table in the sunroom. She might as well be surrounded by blooming plants while doing something unpleasant. She pulled out a chair, sat, opened up the checkbook, and glanced at the amount carried forward in the check register. Not too shabby. Her lips pursed as she considered her aunt's tendency to not record certain things. Agatha, at the bank, phoned whenever an overdraft loomed as a possibility. She retired six months ago, as did the friendly customer service. She closed her eyes, knowing that she'd have to balance the checkbook unaware of when it had last been done.

The phone ringing served as much of a relief as the three o'clock bell on the last day of school, releasing both teachers and students to the summer. "Hello..." Recognizing the number, she added, "...Blue. Got your bull back?"

"I wish. The boys were going to steal him back last night. A couple got scared and backed out. Someone snooping around a property at night can get buckshot."

"You got that right. Not sure why none of you are willing to go up to the front door and ask nicely for your bull back. You *could* press charges."

"Ha! You forget you're not in the city anymore. We don't have any law enforcement. All we have is Miles, who drives the 1960s Mayberry police car he bought at an auction. Technically, since he's not a legal officer, he drives around and wishes everyone a nice day. He shows up at the parade, which is the only time he can use his siren. Even if we had a deputy, it would cause bad feelings if we pressed charges."

"Someone needs to." She growled the words. "It might cause Kevin to stop acting like a fifteen-year-old brat."

"Maybe *you're* the person to do it." Blue exhaled audibly. "Right now, I need to know if Rupert is actually there. I know Griffin thinks he is and my husband doesn't want me to get involved, but there happens to be a school bus/food truck nearby for sale."

"I don't need a food truck."

"It's not an actual food truck. Beth at the bank told me her cousin planned to make it into a food truck, but there's plenty of hoops you have to jump through when selling food to the public. Anyhow, he lost interest. He's into blacksmithing now—fewer rules. Why don't we go see it?"

"Money. I'm trying to make sense of Aunt Cinnamon's checking account right now. Let's just say she believed in creative accounting since she often rounded off the amount she recorded in the register, saying something about it creating a buffer. Unfortunately, she forgot now and then to write in all the checks. It's a bit like a treasure hunt—only there won't be a chest of gold."

"Sounds like you need a break," Blue pointed out. "No one says you have to *buy* the bus. I should be done with milking in about an hour. We'll go for a look, and we'll be close to Kevin's place. It should be easy to pick out Rupert among the mismatched menagerie he has of unwanted animals."

"A break would be nice," she concluded, aware she had failed to even write the first check. She'd best get dressed, knowing Blue probably made the call from the IGA food store parking lot despite her comment about milking. Doubts about the ease of spotting Rupert in a nearby field visited as she levered on her tennis shoes. Driving slowly by Kevin's field and rubbernecking at the animals wouldn't get the job done. She'd bet good money Blue would concoct a dangerous scenario with Tenny being the principal participant.

Chapter Seventeen

A SPRITELY *BEEP beep* signaled Blue's arrival. Tenny pushed the sealed bill payments away from her. Perhaps she could mail them on the way. As soon as she reached for them, she pulled back her hand fast as if burned. What if her latest accounting of the checking account wasn't correct? What if some sizable check Cinnamon had written—but failed to write down—existed out there? The check recipient could have tucked it into a hidden purse pocket before switching purses.

The honk sounded again, ending Tenny's possible scenario of the forgotten check. She erupted into action, scurrying out of the house without the payments. Making sure to lock the door, she turned to wave at Blue, squinting a little in the bright sun. The Moo Town truck served as their stealth vehicle of choice. Surely no one would notice a truck painted to resemble a Holstein cow. "Ah, Blue…" She swung open the passenger door. "…I'm okay with our taking my car. You know, less obvious."

"Maybe so," Blue acknowledged with a nod. "I don't plan on being seen by the practical jokester. He has a day job over in Hamlin. Also, Griffin wants me to pick up some soybean meal and sweet feed."

"Okay. Truck it is. Kevin has an actual adult job?" Her incredulity colored her tone. "Does he work in a novelty shop where he sells hand buzzers and fake packs of gum that snap on your finger when you try to take one?"

"Insurance." Blue shook her head. "Can you imagine his keeping a straight face while quoting statistics about life expectancy and such?"

"Nope." She shook her head, picturing the Kevin she remembered from high school with his wayward mop of orangish-red hair and twinkling blue eyes. However, the twinkle usually came from a prank he'd just set up. No thinking person in Emerson would trust him. "That explains why he works in another town where no one knows him."

Tenny boosted herself into the truck, knowing she'd lost the vehicle battle. Just as well, her compact car was stuffed with items she'd cleared out of her childhood bedroom, intending to take them to Goodwill when she drove into the city. There was no real need for an Easy Bake Oven, Troll dolls, or an Ask Zandar Crystal Ball, which served the same purpose as a Magic Eight Ball. Kids would ask it questions and it usually gave vague answers such as *Ask one of your friends* or *What was the question?* "I'm not sure if there would be room for you between all my old board games and bags of cast-off clothing. I doubt I'll be hosting any game nights with a Hungry, Hungry Hippo game or Old Maid card set."

"Probably not." Blue reversed the truck. "Surprised you still had that stuff. Even in high school, you'd be a little old to play it."

"You'd think that. I occasionally played with Uncle Mark and Aunt Cinnamon. They liked it. I think it made us all feel a little younger."

"I hear you. Still, a game night could be fun. We might need some games aimed at the teens and up category. I have a few. As you know, not much happens in this podunk town."

It was one of the reasons she left, the other being not fitting in—only, she never found that square hole that suited. "Yeah." Remembering her joy teaching some of the younger Emerson residents how a library worked, her tone softened. "I had a young girl a couple of weeks ago that put Podunk in for the name of the town on her library card application. She even asked me how to spell it. After watching her carefully write it, I didn't have the heart to tell her the town's name was Emerson."

They both laughed as Blue shifted into drive and headed north. "You talk to the lawyer yet?"

"No." The question doused the laughter. "I plan to do it today. Not knowing how much money is in the bank makes it hard to pay bills. It would help to know what I have and where it might be tucked away."

Blue slowed for a stop sign but used the pause to direct a long look at Tenny. "Didn't you ask?"

"Of course not." She dug her fingers into her curls and twisted them into a sloppy bun before securing it with a hair tie. "It would make Cinnamon's approaching death more real, more immediate. I didn't want that. When Cinnamon was lucid, I only wanted to discuss good times. Every now and then, she'd throw hints—such as saying things about a box."

"A safety deposit box?" Blue inquired. When another vehicle pulled up behind them, she tapped the gas.

"Hard to say. She didn't call it that. Told me we had stocks and even some bonds. The *good* kind. She said Mark had a knack for that kind of thing." She sighed. "I should have paid more attention, but my emphasis was on her not dying. When I start organizing the house, I might find something."

"Check your key ring and you might find a tiny deposit box key. Then you'll have to figure out the bank, since there are none in Emerson."

She pulled the keys out of her pocket and fingered them. A few small keys poked out between the house keys and car keys. "One I know is for the shed. There's a couple here I have no clue what they're for. I'm sure they'd use the same bank the checking account is at."

"You're halfway there," Blue encouraged. "We're coming up on Kevin's property and your potential food truck bus owner is right next door."

"I don't need a food truck. Just a bookmobile and an affordable one. I'm not sure what I can afford exactly. Wouldn't mind someone giving me a free one. It would make things much less complicated."

"Please." Blue added a derisive snort. "You know better than that. Did you forget everyone is trying to make money somehow by carving mazes in their cornfields, charging people a couple of bucks to view the haunted maze, and then scaring the youngsters by chasing them dressed like a bloody scarecrow?"

"I suspect most of their folks enjoy doing the corn maze. Probably don't turn their noses up at the money, but I get your point."

"I thought you would. Work may need to be done," Blue suggested in a wheedling tone. "You can't expect to find a finished bookmobile for sale. Even if we did, it would cost way more than an old school bus. Remember..." She lengthened the word. "...who promised to help?"

"Dallas. By the way, I have something to tell you." Tenny used her flattened hand as a sun shield over her eyes and read the sign placed over the drive. "Kevin's Menagerie. I thought you made up the name."

"No, it suits. As much as I might want to hate him right now for causing us so much worry with his stupid joke, he *can* be a kind fellow. As you know, most of the 4-H participants auction off the cows, pigs, and sheep they raise. The money goes back into the 4-H organization. The kid whose animal goes for the most gets bragging rights and their name on a plaque. Despite being farm kids, many can't stand the thought of their pig ending up as bacon or their cow being the star of the local barbeque. Kevin's been known to buy a few of those project animals. I suspect he rotates them out."

"What do you mean he rotates them out?" She stared at the field of grazing animals. Cows she recognized immediately, along with a plump Shetland pony. Some long-necked alpacas peered at her over the fence with matching quizzical expressions on their wooly faces.

"Here's the place." The truck turned into a long driveway shaded by red maple trees. In the shade, a brick house remained slightly visible with some odd rounded bump on the side. "As for rotating them out, when a kid quits coming to visit his project animal, the animal may find a home elsewhere."

"Another county?"

"Possibly. More likely a chest freezer. Still, to be fair, Kevin keeps them as long as the child keeps visiting. There she is." Blue slowed the truck and stopped at the red brick home. Next to the house sat a school bus painted brick red. No wonder the house appeared to have a growth on its side. While school bus yellow never did much for her, red failed to create a relaxing attitude conducive to reading. A burnt wood smell clung to it, or possibly, to the house.

As the two of them slid out of the parked truck and moved closer to examine the bus, a screen door slammed. Blue moved closer to Tenny, poking her side with her index finger. "Dallas. Tell me all."

An oversized bear of a man with a full beard that hid the label on the bib of his overalls strolled toward them. His teeth flashed white in his dark beard as he spoke. "Y'all here about the food truck?"

"Bus." Tenny said the word as if it could transform the questionable red food truck bus with a campfire smell into the desired bookmobile.

"Food bus," the would-be mobile restaurateur said. "It sounds a little better. I can get why people want to call it a food bus. Sounds like there might be more food choices or possibly an inside dining area." He interwove his fingers over his rounded stomach, demonstrating his love of cooking and eating. He grimaced. "You might want to take a gander inside before you lean into the dining area." His forehead puckered. "I plumb forgot to introduce myself. Merc. Short for Mercury."

Blue pointed to herself. "Blue, from Moo Town Dairy." She gestured to Tenny. "This is my friend Tenny. You may have known her folks, Mark and Cinnamon. Recently departed."

"Yes, I did." Merc placed an open hand the size of a dinner plate over his heart. "They were good people."

"They were," she agreed, noticing what Blue was doing, working in the sympathy angle. Part of her mind still played with the thought of a dining area, which readers wouldn't need. All the same, she'd planned on looking inside even though she hadn't any big plans on getting the bus. The price would determine her interest. "Can we walk through the bus?"

"Absolutely," Merc assured and led them to the doors, prying them open by slipping his hands between the folding doors and pulling them open. The wood smoke smell intensified.

Not exactly secure, she thought as she inched closer and stepped on the first step. She paused, closed her eyes for a second, and then opened them, hoping for the big reveal effect. *Nothing.* Well, not exactly nothing, just *mostly* nothing, with the exception of blackness coating the ceiling, the floors, the walls, and no bus seats. In the very back, a couple of large, bullet-shaped objects took up most of the space. "What's that in the back?"

Merc chuckled. "You don't know your way around a grill. That's a smoker. Two, to be exact. I had a couple of wood and fire grills in here, too. Not my best decision."

The blackness, she understood. To test her theory, Tenny touched the wall with two fingers and they came back sooty. *Good grief.* Just a little soot inside a candle jar ended up taking much more time than it should to clean. A bus might take a year or more. There was no need to even ask what he wanted, since Tenny knew this would be a no-go. She held up her fingers for Blue to see the result.

Her friend surprised her by saying, "Merc, we need to take some time to talk this over. Maybe we'll head over to the fence line for privacy?"

"Take all the time you need," Merc assured them with a pleased grin.

Before Tenny could question her friend's sanity, Blue grabbed her arm as soon as both feet touched the ground and pulled her toward Kevin's farm. She waited until they were out of hearing range and almost at the fence line before declaring, "I don't want that bus!"

"Who would?" Blue acknowledged and waved a hand in front of her face. "It stinks. Not to mention he's ruined it with his barbequing. It might not even run anymore. He's lucky he didn't blow the whole thing up."

"I'm glad you agree with me." Tenny glanced back to the bus where the owner waited, leaning against the object in question. "So, why did we have to run over here to talk?"

"Wait." Blue patted down her jeans pockets and withdrew a small pair of binoculars. "We're here to find Rupert, or at least evidence he's at Kevin's." She fiddled with the control dial, sharpening the focus. "I think I see something." She inhaled sharply. "That dirty dog."

Without another word, Blue dropped the binoculars, pulled two strands of barbed wire apart, and ducked through the fence. For a few seconds, Tenny watched slacked-mouthed as her friend ran across the pasture, dodging the occasional goat or llama. Did she totally forget about just *getting* proof?

With the forgotten binoculars lying on the ground, Tenny picked them up and peered through them. Looking through both her glasses and the binoculars made everything a little fuzzy. Tucking her regular glasses into her shirt collar, she tried the binoculars again. She saw grazing cows of all sorts, a pony, and alpacas or llamas—it was hard to remember which was which. Blue was headed to the far field where a behemoth of a beast grazed. However, that wasn't Rupert. "Wait!"

Chapter Eighteen

NOT EXPERIENCED IN handling livestock or barbed wire fences, Tenny plucked at the fence, unsure of how to surmount it. She shot a glance back at the house, hoping the oversized bus salesman would lend a hand. He could probably throw her in the field with ease. It could be he couldn't see her under the shadows of the nearby tree. "It's up to me…" She hoped the words would inspire. They didn't.

She stared at the fence. While she couldn't pull the barbed wires apart and slip through them, she knelt beside the fence, inspecting the lowest wire, which stretched about a foot or more from the ground. No help for it, she flattened herself against the grass and rotted leaves, using her elbow to propel her as she army crawled into the field. Her skinny body, which earned her more than her share of teasing with names like bean pole or stick figure in gym class, served her well. She put down her hands to push upright, only to find them planted in mud—she hoped it was mud. Wincing, she wiped her hands on the grass and then darted across the field in an ungainly run while yelling, "Blue! Blue! It's not a bull!"

A few grazing cows glanced at her as she trotted by, and a trio of small goats shadowed her. How could her friend not notice the large hump on the animal, signifying it wasn't Rupert? The only cow breed she knew about having a hump was the Brahman breed, which usually existed in much hotter climates. Her goat friends danced around her as if involved in a game that Tenny had somehow initiated. When she paused to use her flattened hand as a sunshade to determine Blue's location, one of the goats butted her. "Stop that!"

Being a goat, it kept on butting her—nothing too hard, but annoying, especially as she searched for her friend. The sun overhead threw shadows around the barns and nearby corrals. One corral held the silhouette of what she knew to be a bison. How could a woman who worked with cows every day make such a mistake? Inhaling, she readied herself to run up the hill and rescue her bestie before she climbed into the corral with the bison. Another headbutt, this one stronger, sent Tenny sprawling. Small hooves attached to gangly legs and hairy compact bodies with cute goat heads clambered over her.

"Off! Off!" She accompanied the words with pushing until cleared of the last goat and stood up. "Geesh. It's no wonder you're here."

A metallic groan brought Tenny's attention back to the bison enclosure—without the bison. It was just an empty corral and an open gate. Standing close to six feet, with all four hooves on the ground, it wasn't hard to locate the massive critter. The shaggy-headed behemoth grazed not far from the open gate, enjoying the opportunity for a fresh bit of grass. Blue stood near the gate, waving both arms, warning Tenny a killing machine had wandered into the pasture. Well aware of the nature of such a creature since she covered the dangers in her fifth-grade report on Yellowstone Park, she froze. Part of her brain screamed *run*, but another part debated if running wouldn't attract the loose animal's interest. There was a sound very far away—she recognized Blue's voice, but couldn't understand what she was saying. Her breath quickened as her eyes remained on the hairy grazer. On the surface, it acted rather mellow. Her reference librarian brain opened a file labeled *bison attacks*.

Depending on the source, sixty reported attacks were usually tourists wanting to get a selfie with the big mammals. Not too surprisingly, the bison wasn't a fan of flash photography. Those with young reacted strongly. Some even charged cars. With that in mind, maybe it wouldn't even notice a skinny, slow-moving human. A hand landed on her arm, stopping her heart for the briefest moment until she realized it was Blue. Bison legs ended in hooves, not hands.

The breath she'd been holding expelled with a whoosh. She covered Blue's hand with her own. "I was so afraid for you."

Blue cocked her head like a curious puppy, her brow wrinkling. "Why?"

"Ah, large dangerous mammal over here." She angled her head to where Hairy McScary chewed.

"Oh, him. He's ancient. Kevin bought him off a sideshow. You've probably seen the signs along the highway to see an actual bison. He's harmless."

"Harmless?" She doubted that. After all, she'd read plenty on bison and bison attacks at national parks. "Why was he separated from the other animals if he's as gentle as a lamb?"

"I didn't say gentle..." Blue hooked her arm around Tenny's waist and turned her toward the fence. "We need to move slowly and confidently across the field. No sudden movements."

They crept across the field. Tenny kept a close eye on where she stepped. A wrong step in a cow pie would send her to the ground and not so silently. "Problem is..." Blue whispered. "...not so much us, but Billy the Bison. I imagine most of the cows are used to humans. No big deal. They might even be used to Billy behind a fence. What they aren't used to is Billy the Bison in the field with them."

Paradoxically, the fence moved farther away—or at least it seemed like it. Even though she knew better than to ask, Tenny wondered aloud, "What might the cows do when they see Billy in the field with them?"

"Depends. At the current time, he's not charging, bellowing, or running around the field like a wild animal. It should be fine, or not."

The *or not* failed to instill confidence, but at least the fence line remained stationary as opposed to moving. Almost there, they could do it. "Should I know about the *or not*?"

"Maybe." Blue tightened her grip on her friend's waist. "It's always better to be prepared."

"Boy Scout motto," Tenny quipped, aware she rambled when anxious.

"Grandmother." Blue clarified, then cleared her throat. "Cows are simple creatures who react. Sometimes, one cow might react to a bee and kick out, and the next cow does likewise. What we need to worry about is a stampede."

"Stampede?" Images of hundreds of cows thundering over the plain came to mind. Alongside them, handsome cowboys on quarter horses did their best to turn the mob. The scenario shouldn't apply here. "He only has a handful of cows, not even a dozen."

"They can still stampede. Depending on the cow, anything can startle it—a car backfiring, fireworks, or even a horse harassing a single cow. Most people aren't aware that horses can be jerks sometimes."

"Yeah, jerks. Rather like some goats I've encountered." Even though the fence loomed only ten feet away, Tenny swiveled her head, speculating on her cloven-hooved nemeses' location. The frolicking goats jumped and cavorted in the tall grass not more than three feet from Billy the Bison. "Ah, Blue…"

A low, gravely roar erupted and a few alarmed cow calls followed. Before Tenny could gauge what havoc the goats caused, Blue grabbed her hand and shouted, "Run!"

Thundering hooves gathered in volume as they sprinted to the fence. Blue dropped her hand, grabbed onto the fence post, put her foot on the first wire, and scrambled over the fence, ripping the seat of her jeans in the process.

A backward glance determined the cows' closeness, along with a few trailing llamas at the rear of the group. Blue held wide the two wires, and Tenny dived through them just as the mini herd ran by. Stunned, she lay on the ground in a fetal position until Blue nudged her with the toe of her boot.

"You okay?"

Hearing the concern in her friend's voice, Tenny rolled to a sitting position before answering. "A little rattled. Stampedes tend to do that to me."

"I can see that." Blue pointed to the field where the cows milled a bit before going back to eating grass. "Look, they stopped. Good deal. Sometimes, cows can run for miles when stampeding. Generally, they don't, but it's hard to stop when you have running bovines packed on all sides of you. Fortunately, Kevin has enough space and a limited number of cows, making stopping no problem. I guess I should call Kevin."

"Really?" Tenny puckered her mouth as if biting into an unripe persimmon. "I thought he was the enemy."

"No." Blue shook her head and gave a slight shrug of her shoulders. "I checked his barn. No sign of Rupert. We can't be mad about something he didn't do."

"Good point."

The black and white Moo Town truck shimmered under the noonday sun like a sanctuary. All they'd have to do was climb inside and be gone. Everything else today would be easy after almost getting stampeded. On her feet again, Tenny brushed at her clothes and realized the futility of her efforts. Blue pulled her phone out and scrolled through it before pushing a number and then waited.

"Hey, Kevin. I'm at your neighbor's, looking at his food truck."

A silence ensued at Blue's end, meaning Kevin must be talking.

"Oh, no. It's not for me. Tenny. It's for Tenny. Anyhow, we noticed your bison is in with the cows. I didn't know if that is the way you want it or what."

There was another silence on Blue's end, and then, "Oh, really? Will do. Bye now."

Curious about the conversation, Tenny demanded, "What did he say?"

Blue held up one finger. "Get this. He told me to tell his neighbor, the Barbeque King, to sing the bison back up to his corral. Billy the Bison appreciates his singing."

Chapter Nineteen

CLOUDS GATHERED TOGETHER as if sharing a secret, dimming the sunlight as Blue and Tenny drove back to town. Her ever-optimistic friend remained silent, white-knuckling the steering wheel. Tenny reached up to push a curl behind her ear as she contemplated her friend's mood. Blue had counted on her bull being at Kevin's, all safe and sound. Knowing as far as solutions went, Tenny had none, her friendship demanded she offer anyhow. "Umm, is there anything I can do?"

"I don't know." One hand went up to wipe away a tear. "Griffin will be devastated. Of course, we had Rupert insured. Still, it's not the same. It took years to build up his reputation. In some ways, he was our farm's mascot. Rupert, the gentleman bull." She sniffed. "Tell me something else to distract me."

What a tall order! The newly cut fields surrounding the fair-grounds and the carnival rides half assembled caught Tenny's attention. She cleared her throat. "Last night, I was taking a cool bath, face mask, cucumbers on my eyes—the whole bit."

"Glad you had a spa day, but as distracting topics go, that's not working. I can still see a confused Rupert in a strange stall, wondering why we abandoned him."

"Wait!" Tenny held up her hand, halting whatever Blue might

say next. "It gets better. I'm in the tub relaxing when I hear the doorbell ring. I think door-to-door salesman, but then we don't have door-to-door salesmen because we aren't close to anything."

"Tangent…" Blue pointed out the obvious. "Cut to the chase."

"Okay." She inhaled and said quickly, "Dallas asked me to the fair while I was in Uncle Mark's ratty robe, a shower cap, and a green face mask. He asked what night. I told him the sheepdog herding night and then one of my neighbors walked by and called me a zombie."

Blue whistled. "You *did* cut to the chase. Green face, ratty robe, zombie. Not your typical romantic meet-cute." She turned slightly toward Tenny and slowed her speed. Her eyebrows arched as she announced, "You know, Rita's going to lay an egg over this."

"Rita! Rita! Rita! Why does everything have to revolve around her?"

"You have been gone for a while." Blue wrinkled her nose and pushed out a humorless laugh. "Everything revolves around Rita because that's what she wants. If her daddy doesn't use his power on the town council to get what his baby wants, she bats her lash extensions at someone who will. Last time someone told her *no* was the Widow McClintock. Her son joined the service, leaving behind the prettiest little palomino filly."

"Butterscotch…" Tenny supplied the name. "A real beauty with an elegant gait. I can see why Rita would want her. Probably felt like one beautiful blonde deserves another."

"Sounds like something she'd say. Anyhow, Rita and her daddy headed to the widow's house to put a bid on the horse."

"I bet she wasn't selling it."

"Oh, she was selling it—not to Rita, though. She even comment-ed she wouldn't do that to the horse. It ended in Rita having a falling-on-the-ground tantrum like a two-year-old. Only, she was twenty-two."

Tenny snorted, trying to imagine the stylish woman throwing herself on the ground. She must have dressed appropriately if a tantrum served as one of her options. "Did she end up with Butterscotch?"

"No. A sweet little girl in the next county got her. She shows her all the time and has placed more than once."

Tenny clapped her hands together. "Good for the girl and Butterscotch." Her pleased expression vanished as she inquired, "How did Rita and company punish Widow McClintock for standing her ground?"

"Well," Blue hesitated as she turned down Main Street. "That's another story. She died shortly after that. Fell down an open well on her property."

"Seriously?" Tenny cocked her head and regarded her friend with disbelief. "Surely the widow would know where an open well was on her property and how to avoid it."

"Yep," Blue acknowledged, guiding the truck into the spot in front of Tenny's home. "Everyone pointed out that it happened right after she sold Butterscotch to someone else."

"Rita? Her father?" Gossip served as one of their favorite pastimes in Emerson. What people didn't know, they made up. "Did no one do anything?"

"What could they do?" Her shoulders hunched up in a shrug. "Rumors and conjecture. Not enough to bring in the law. Her son came home to handle everything, and he failed to sound the alarm. Why should anyone else?"

Tenny pushed up her slipping glasses with one finger. "This is your tale about the last person who stood up to Rita, and your point is?"

"Plenty of people had their suspicions. Elmer, who worked as a handyman for the widow, pointed out that a concrete slab usually rested over the played-out well. The day the accident happened, the slab had been moved. It weighed two or three hundred pounds. Not something a frail senior could push or lift. Anyhow, my point is plenty of people blamed Rita. Not to her face, of course. She doesn't even discourage people because she likes people being scared of her and scurrying around to do her bidding, afraid they might end up in a well."

"Wow! I always knew she was a bully." Tenny rested her hand on the interior truck handle. "Maybe I should pass on my fair date."

Blue leaned over to grasp her departing friend's arm. "Don't you dare! Maybe Dallas is the right person for you and you can make him happy. Are you saying Dallas doesn't deserve happiness?"

"Talk about overkill." She glanced at her friend's hand still gripping her arm. "I'm worried about Rita stirring up trouble for *me*."

"I can see that." Blue dropped her hand and held up a finger. "What can she do to you? Your family is gone. No more library. It's not like she's going to break up a non-existent romance. Quite frankly, you have nothing left to lose."

Good friends, while often great with straight talk, often mishandled the tact factor. "Thanks, I guess. I'll keep you informed about the date."

"Wear something cute," Blue advised with a grin.

Glad her friend's mood had lifted, she teased back, "I'm just not sure which book T-shirt is the flirtiest." On that note, she slid out of the truck and waved. "See ya."

A quick tap on the horn served as Blue's reply as she reversed and headed out.

Chapter Twenty

A RUSTLING ON the porch had Tenny turning slowly, but seeing nothing, she continued toward the front door. It was best to get inside and paw through her meager wardrobe for a date-appropriate outfit. Plenty of glossy fashion magazines would advise a short dress with high heels as the way to go. With her height, she'd earn a comparison to a giraffe. For those who were quick with the nicknames, she'd become *giraffe legs* or some other awkward label. As for the heels, she would probably pierce the grass, serving as a human aerator. Humidity made the door stick, earning a shoulder bump, which sent it swinging wide enough for Precious to shoot through.

"Precious!" she yelled as the critter darted under a tablecloth-draped side table. "Just what I need."

She slammed the door but moved past the table where Precious hid. Her four legged sibling was more agile than she was. She chased, he evaded. Tenny called, Precious ignored. Doing something that might interest the raccoon, such as making his favorite meals, could lure him out of concealment. He might even be hungry.

Tenny reached her bedroom and pulled her closet door wide. There were navy cardigans, khaki pants, white blouses, and numerous clever shirts with bookish sayings such as *Books are your best defense against unwanted conversation.* While it made her smile, it wouldn't be much of a date if neither of them spoke. A quick visit to a nearby town's discount store might yield her something both pretty and charming or, at the very least, more colorful. On the way, she could stop by the lawyer's office. First, she'd have to get Precious out of the house.

After whipping up a quick meal of scrambled eggs that Precious wolfed down, she lured him out of the house with a hefty slice of pineapple upside-down cake. Tenny grabbed her purse with intentions of shopping. "You're a fortunate fellow since I don't share my favorite cake with just anyone."

Precious used both hands to shove the tasty dessert into his face, failing to react to Tenny's words. "Oh well. I'm off. You might want to nap while I'm gone." With a skip in her step, she hurried down the sidewalk to the garage where her loaded car waited for her. At least she'd get the stuff dropped off.

Slipping behind the steering wheel of her car brought her a sense of ease. The car gurgled to life, and she pushed in her Moby CD, rolled down the windows and drove. A sense of lightness accompanied her each mile farther from town—no Rita issues, no bull thieves, and no one trying to sell her an overpriced bus in questionable condition.

Cinnamon's lawyer operated out of his home, stating he saw no reason to keep a town office, or town hours. A white-washed Lincoln fence surrounded the landscaped property. Pine trees bookended the rambling ranch. A blue compact in the driveway signaled someone was at home. Fortune must be with her that someone would be here when she had finally worked up the gumption to stop by. Another brick in the wall or, more likely, another step closer to her future, whatever that might be.

Her knock sounded soft even to Tenny's ears, but the door swung open, revealing a bright-eyed Philomena, the lawyer's wife and primo gossip, dressed in a ruffled chicks and hen apron. "I saw you pull in and I bet I know why you're here!"

With anyone else, it might sound like some type of street fortune telling, but with Philomena's connections, she usually did know ahead of time. "Um, hello. Why am I here?"

"You came to ask my husband about your aunt's will."

She had to give it to Philomena. "You're right about that."

"Before you ask, DH is not home. That stands for dear husband, you know. My favorite character in my daytime story uses that to refer to her spouse. I figure if it's good enough for her, then…"

Tenny cleared her throat, well aware that once Philomena went off on a tangent, it would be a good ten minutes before coming to the point.

"Oh, right." She crinkled her nose. "He's still on his fishing trip, but I will remind him to call you as soon as he gets home."

"I'd appreciate it."

Tenny turned to leave when Philomena called out, "Where you off to?"

No way. She would not get pulled in by the woman's congenial manner and have her business spread all over town. "Errands. I have a ton of them. See you."

The nearest town of Beechnut only numbered a thousand or more souls than Emerson, but they more than made up for it in stores. They had three groceries. Plus, one carried clothes and other household items. A dry cleaner, two hardware stores, a Goodwill, four mechanics, a dozen assorted restaurants—most being the fast-food sort—and a small second-run theatre rounded out the offerings. Sprinkled in between, a shifting collection of small boutiques popped up, offering everything from porcelain collectibles to gifts with cutesy country sayings. Once on a trip with her aunt before her health failed, an upscale consignment store existed. Maybe it might still be around and, even better, have an outfit that trod the thin line between being flirty, but not too outrageous that she'd make it on the gossip top five. Just being seen with Dallas would pop her into the top ten. He epitomized the boy next door, and his brief association with Rita, earned him a wounded warrior designation from all who'd experienced the queen of mean up close and personal.

After dropping off her donations at Goodwill, she slowly drove through the streets of Beechnut, trying to remember where she'd seen the consignment shop. With the posted speed limit of twenty-five miles per hour, her crawl through the streets wouldn't attract attention. Traffic slowed near the fast-food restaurants as cars turned into the already full drive-thrus. Her stomach grumbled, reminding her that while Precious had eaten, she hadn't. The idea of not eating the days-old food waiting for her at home appealed. Most of the refrigerated and all the frozen food would still be edible. Despite Cinnamon's close friends scoring ribbons at the fair's annual bake-off, sadness flavored the recipes. Sure, she knew it was a matter of perception. It turned out her perception influenced her taste buds.

A burger, fries, and possibly a milkshake sang their siren song, drawing her closer. There used to be a place with excellent fried fish that her uncle preferred. The restaurants crowded together on the main strip, their neon signs vying for prominence like weeds on a highway shoulder. It made it hard to distinguish separate entrances. Tenny recognized the blue and white décor of the seafood kitchen and made a right turn into the busy lot.

Everyone must have dropped everything and rushed to grab lunch. Surely someone would pull out. A couple exited the building and headed toward their cars. Tenny braked and waited. The woman's confident stride reminded her of someone. Wait a minute! She tipped down her prescription sunglasses, rubbed her eyes, and pushed them back up. Rita! She wouldn't be caught dead in a fast-food restaurant—or at least that's what she would always say. Who was the man? As if on cue, he turned slightly and waved goodbye before disappearing inside an F-450 truck big enough to haul a fifth-wheel camper with ease.

He *was* familiar looking. Without Blue beside her to rattle off names, she scoured her mind for the right moniker. The truck engine growled and released a puff of black smoke before easing out of the space. A large magnetic sign hung on the side of the door advertising *Darling Dairies*. Of course! It was Rand Darling. Before she could ease into the empty space, Rita reversed fast, almost hitting Tenny with her Mercedes. Rita sped out of the parking lot as if trying to shake off the ordinary feeling such a place might convey.

Tenny slid into the empty parking place and pulled out her phone. Surely her friend would love to hear about Rand and Rita meeting for lunch. Apparently, Rand had lost his nerd image when he shortened his name and became the biggest dairy operation in Emerson. While Rita might consider the single man as a dating hopeful, she kept it quiet by meeting him in Beechnut. Knowing how she hated people speculating about her, Tenny pushed the phone back into her purse. There was no reason to spread gossip since it grew on its own naturally.

After a crispy white fish sandwich and fries, Tenny used her phone for the address of the consignment shop. It was only a couple of blocks away, which tempted her to walk, but she didn't, since the restaurant needed every single space. While driving, she noticed chrome display racks loaded with clothes nestled in front of the boutique. A bright hand-painted wooden sign with a yellow duck on it identified it as *Lucky Duck Consignments.*

The Rita sighting had her glancing over her shoulder as she exited her car, as though Rita might pop up out of the ground like the varmint in the Whack-A-Mole game. *Get a grip. No one could pay Rita enough to be this close to a consignment shop.*

Relieved, she exhaled, unaware she'd been holding her breath. A middle-aged woman stepped out of the shop attired in a lime green jacket worn over a floral sundress. A coordinating scarf held back her highlighted curls. She smiled at Tenny. "Beautiful day."

"Yes, it is," Tenny agreed, liking the woman immediately.

"Are you looking for something for a special event?"

While she recognized the query as standard sales patter, she realized with surprise she *did* have a special event. "Yes, I am. I have a date for the county fair. My goal is to be cute but practical as I work my way around the straw, sawdust, and everything else."

The woman chuckled. "You've come to the right place. By the way, I'm Emma Jean and I own the shop." She gave Tenny a long, head-to-toe look. "Hey, aren't you Cinnamon's girl?"

"I am." While most people might graciously tell each other they hadn't changed a bit, Tenny realized she pretty much resembled her senior photo, which wasn't necessarily a good thing.

"Well then..." Emma Jean motioned her inside. "...I've got

something special for you. No sidewalk clearances for *you*."

"Um…" Tenny hesitated, glancing at the racks and *very* affordable prices on the cardboard over the rounders. "There might be something I like outside."

"There isn't," Emma Jean assured. "Everything worth having is gone. All that's left are the clothes no one in Beechnut wants, which is saying something because it takes a while for fashion to reach us. Don't worry about the price either. It's the very least I can do for Cinnamon, especially since I missed her service." She grimaced. "It was awful. I was on an Alaskan cruise. My husband, Jimmy, kept promising he'd take me on one. If I'd known Cinnamon would go while I was on vacation, I'd not have gone."

"You know my aunt—she'd have wanted you to go." Tenny stepped inside and turned slowly, taking in the rows of jeans, skirts, jackets, and dresses. Corners were dedicated to jewelry, shoes, and accessories. She placed both hands on her hips. "Show me what you've got."

Chapter Twenty-One

T HE SCENT OF kettle corn and hot grease used to fry elephant's ears hung in the air. Loud rock music carried from the midway, interrupted with calls from the PA system for the participants in the confirmation class for market pigs to report to the swine judging area. People hurried by her house, chattering excitedly as they made their way to the fairgrounds. Some parked on the street for ease of leaving. Others chose the town streets because they refused to pay the five dollars for parking that benefited the local 4-H organization, which was the whole reason they even had a fair. Tenny stepped outside, put both hands on her hips, and surveyed the clouds that gathered ominously over the fairgrounds. Rain would arrive before the night did.

Any other day, the sun seared the landscape, but on the days that she ran a special defrizzing gel through her curls, it would always rain. The expensive hair product she'd convinced herself to buy tamed her curls into smooth ringlets for now. Humidity would make her hair double in size. Tenny patted her hair and hoped her date ended before the inevitable showers.

With that in mind, she scampered into the house to get ready. Emma Jean, the boutique owner, convinced Tenny a pair of low-heeled cowboy boots served as a must for the fair, along with a reasonable length jean skirt paired with a green plaid blouse. Even though the shop owner included a straw cowboy hat with the ensemble, Tenny left it on the bed. Everything about her outfit existed outside of her comfort zone. Maybe in a year or two she'd try the hat.

A dab of lip gloss, a brush of mascara, and a spritz of perfume equated to full makeup—and just in time, too. Dallas called through the screen door, "Anybody home?"

Tenny walked slowly out of the bedroom, hidden in the shadows until she reached the living room where she twirled and answered. "I'm ready!"

"Yes, you are," Dallas agreed, opening the screen door. "Let's go. Sheepdog herding is popular. We'll have to hurry if we want to grab a seat. Otherwise, we'll end up standing for the duration. Besides," he grinned as he added, "I want to show you off."

The possibility both excited and alarmed her. Outside of her diorama skills, she'd never been shown off. Grabbing her purse, she stepped out onto the porch, joining Dallas. She locked the door to keep Precious and any other varmints out. "I'm not sure how I feel about being shown off."

Dallas held out his bent arm for her to rest her hand on as if they were a celebrity couple walking the red carpet. The polished square toes of rancher boots peeked out from Dallas' jeans, confirming boots as the correct shoe choice. Surprisingly, he'd chosen a red plaid shirt, making them both appear as a cover couple for the Christmas edition of *The Modern Farmer's Digest*.

"Not much you can do about it." He winked. "I like your hair down. I had no clue it was past your shoulders."

"It surprised me, too, since I have it either in a bun or ponytail."

She shrugged her shoulders. "Thanks," she murmured. "I guess I should have led with that."

"No problem. I also heard they have deep-fried brownies and a loaded corn dog, which is a corn dog with a dollop of macaroni and cheese on top. Decide what you want to eat and if you want to eat before or after you go on the tilt-a-whirl ride." Dallas was in a teasing mode as they strolled down the sidewalk.

"Tilt-a-whirl…" Tenny repeated the name of the iconic round car ride that traveled over a shifting track, spinning madly in circles and dashing riders against each other. Most young male teens loved this ride for its wildness and the possibility of brushing up against their crush. It was not as big a favorite with older folks, who complained it just made them nauseous. While Tenny had certainly passed the teenage years, she hadn't yet reached the uneasy stomach age. At least, she didn't think she had. All the same, it would be better to be safe. "Eating is something we can do last."

A thin rope fence encircled the parking area. Dallas hopped over and held out his hand for Tenny as she carefully stepped over the fence without showing too much skin. A couple of local church ladies spotted Tenny and waved.

The one with a halo of white gossamer hair and sporting a shirt with a pig on it with the various cuts denoted by dotted lines called out, "It's so nice you're getting out!"

"I can't miss the fair!" Tenny forced a smile, aware she could be trapped in a long conversation with a woman whose name she couldn't remember.

"I hear you," the companion to the first lady acknowledged. She patted her unnaturally bright red hair and sniffed. "It won't be the same without your aunt's cinnamon rolls. No one held a candle to her baking."

"So true," Tenny concurred, casting an imploring glance at Dallas. He certainly didn't ask for this interruption to their date.

"Ah, Miss Eloise, Miss June." Dallas identified the women by name, something she hadn't been able to do. He flashed the gorgeous smile that had always made Tenny's heart flutter. The women's happy faces showed that his charm worked on all ages. "I hate to interrupt such a nice visit, but my date and I need to get to the sheepdog herding show before the seats are gone."

Gossamer hair responded first. "Oh my. I had no clue, Dallas. I thought you were just working the parking lot." She made a shooing motion with her hands. "You two, go on!"

"Good luck!" the red-headed woman called after them as they worked their way between cars and headed toward concrete block buildings named after the four pillars of 4-H—Heart, Head, Hands, and Health.

Dallas pointed to the right. "I heard it's in the Heart building."

Only half-listening, Tenny peeped at the church women whispering behind them. "Why do you think she said good luck? It's like she knew something. That's the kind of thing you say when someone announces they're going to jump out of a plane."

Dallas reached for her hand, entwining his fingers with hers and waited for a reaction. When Tenny lifted one eyebrow, he laughed. "You knew when you agreed to this date there would be talk. There's *always* talk. I figured I should make my intentions clear."

"That you have." The oversized moths that sometimes took residence in her belly flapped their sizable wings. Part of her believed this was all just a wonderful fantasy. Even now, she might be fast asleep in Uncle Mark's striped hammock tied underneath the elm tree.

"As I live and breathe!" Rita's overloud and dramatic voice cut through the noise. "Who's Dallas slumming with?"

Even though her first intention should be to take cover, Tenny froze in place, realizing in the space of a held breath that she wasn't asleep and why the church lady had wished her good luck. At that moment, she would have given anything to be in her safe hammock alternative.

Dallas tugged her hand. "Let's go." He guided her into the Heart building, refusing to greet his ex-wife. Once they'd found a place on the upper bleachers, Tenny whispered, "She'll make you pay for ignoring her. There are a lot of things Rita hates, but not being the center of attention is the one thing she hates the most."

"I know," Dallas replied with a knowing smile and a head nod. "Besides, I doubt she can do much more to me than she's already done. I'm more worried about you."

"Sweet." She nudged her date as five sheep reluctantly entered the fenced-in area while excited dogs sat next to their individual owners, trembling with excitement. "The show is about ready to start. Besides, she didn't even recognize me. All the better."

Chapter Twenty-Two

TIRED SHEEP EMITTED grumpy *baas* as a lab shepherd mix herded them into their fenced enclosure on the far side of the ring. Applause rewarded the performance along with a snack slipped to the dog by its owner. Pushed wide, the open exterior doors allowed the last of the setting sun to add a golden softness to the scene. The galvanized bleachers Tenny perched upon groaned when anyone moved, making her a tad uneasy. Sure, the hard bench left a lot to be desired as far as comfort, but maybe the thought of Rita somewhere stirring up trouble fostered her anxiety. Despite her bold words to Blue about having nothing Rita could ruin since everything of value to her had already faded away, she wouldn't want to test her theory. Her eyes cut to Dallas, whose sun-browned face crinkled into happy lines as he grinned.

"I kind of feel sorry for the sheep," Tenny admitted, feeling like the moment called for her to say something—and definitely *nothing* about Rita. While she never considered herself much of a dater, she had garnered a few tidbits from overheard conversations in the library and break room. One of the main complaints of both men and women was the mention of an ex while on a date. It turned the couple into an awkward trio. Just the mention of the ex brought another person to the date, if only in both participants' minds.

Perhaps the woman might question if she were as attractive as the previous ex—a big *no* in her case, but her aunt often repeated that the more you got to know a person's character, they either became more attractive or less, depending on what you uncovered.

Dallas, unaware of Tenny's thoughts, nodded. "The sheep might get a workout today, but most days they just graze." The benches groaned as people stood to leave as a black and white border collie took first place. "Ready to hit the midway?" Dallas inquired.

The midway with the rides, lights, and music rated as a teen hangout and occasionally young families strolled through, their small children begging for the stuffed animals at the various game booths—unaware that the money spent to win one could buy a dozen at a local discount store. Most parents caved and did try the games, only to walk away with a minuscule prize.

Where would Rita be? If she couldn't be the 4-H queen—and she couldn't, because not only had she been it once, but currently she was just too old—that must burn. Since attention worked as her drug of choice, she'd probably stroll slowly by the carnies, allowing them to get an eyeful of what they could never have. "I want to see the exhibits with the flowers, models, photography, and stuff."

"Really?" Dallas cocked his head as if trying to figure out her choice.

"Yeah," she reassured. "You know I'm a sucker for a good diorama."

"Who could forget?" He scrambled to his feet, stretched, and then offered a hand to Tenny. As they exited the building, Dallas greeted folks by name, and occasionally inquired about their family, crops, or their litter of blue tick hound puppies.

Even though his father had moved here initially to pastor a

church, Dallas certainly had planted some deep roots. It was sad. Tenny tried to tamp down the thought of relocation. Being a farmer was who he was. Sure, it would be easy to move somewhere else, but why should he?

The PA burst into action with a shrill sound and then a throat clearing. "Spring Dairy Heifer Class Level 1 proceed to the cattle barn ring. Level 2 participants, time to put the final touches on your heifers."

A few grade school kids kitted out in their best dress jeans and western wear grasped the halters of their heifers, which outweighed them by a few hundred pounds. Parents called out pose suggestions as they shot pictures on their cell phones. Dallas touched her arm and indicated the young 4-H members. "Want to go watch?"

Normally, she would. But not today. "Reminds me too much of Rupert and everything Blue and Griffin are going through." She sighed and glanced up at her date. "I wish I could help somehow." Her lips twisted as she contemplated revealing her one tiny piece of evidence. "However, I did find something in the field that might help. Do you know if Griffin called the police?"

"He should have." Dallas' left hand slipped up and cupped the back of his neck. "Of course, you know all we have is a sheriff and a half-dozen deputies for the entire county." He dropped his hand and moved his head closer. "What did you find?"

Not knowing who she could trust, Tenny motioned to an area right outside the cow wash stands which, while muddy, stood empty. Maneuvering around puddles, they found a dry patch where Tenny pulled out her phone and revealed the tire tread photo. "Look. We found this impression next to the fence. Blue says it doesn't belong to any of their vehicles."

Dallas took the phone and enlarged the photo. He frowned as he turned it one way, then another. "Big truck. Big tires. Could be almost anyone who owns an F-350 or bigger—a standard truck for hauling a horse trailer, camper, or boat."

"What about the notch in the tread?" She pointed to the space on the tire image.

"Those are Water King brands—especially good in the rain. The deep treads channel away the water and mud. What looks like a notch is actually the letter W. It's just branding. I've got the same tires on the truck I use to haul my boat."

The photo had created a kernel of hope that somehow it would lead them to the bull-napper. "Oh." Her shoulders sagged along with her attitude. "I kind of hoped it would be the smoking gun, so to speak."

"Wait!" He examined the photo again. "Whoops, I was wrong." He pointed to the notch again. "I thought this was a W for Water King, but it's an M for Water Master."

Someone in tire land certainly enjoyed creating semi-mythological sounding names for their products. While part of her understood Dallas' need to make her feel better about her foray into sleuthing, she didn't understand the reason behind the names. "This makes a difference how?"

"Around here, most people find it hard to justify buying Water King, especially if not on sale, but Water Master is even more expensive. Not sure if I even know anyone who would fork over the big bucks for that. It must be an outsider." He shook his head slowly. "I just don't understand the why."

A quicksilver possibility occurred and then left as fast as it came as the PA burbled to life. "Make your way to the Hands building!

We're ready to hand out the blue ribbons for best yeast rolls."

Excited murmurs sounded and part of the crowd surged in that direction. Tenny closed her eyes, inhaling deeply and wondering why everything the PA squawked came with emotional baggage. In the past, she'd already be at the building, applauding hard for her relative. She noticed Dallas watching her intently.

"Something wrong?"

"In a way." Her eyes dropped to her mud-dabbed boots. Sharing her innermost feelings wasn't something she did much. Maybe she should take a chance. Her gaze lifted as she spoke. "Any other year, Uncle Mark and I would be waiting for Aunt Cinnamon to accept the ribbon with a gracious thank you. Strangely, she always acted surprised when she won, despite the fact that she kept tweaking her recipe to stay ahead of the competition."

"I guess you want to bypass the ceremony."

She blew out a breath. "I do, but I won't. My aunt would want me to congratulate the yeast roll winner. That's what *she* would do."

"Okay! Let's go." Dallas offered his bent arm. They tread carefully over the muddy ground, slipping every now and then, causing Tenny to catch her breath and only releasing it once they reached the safety of the paved sidewalk.

"I'm not sure I'd have made it on my own. Thanks." As they headed to the Hands building, she thought she spotted Rita and her cohort slipping into the edifice. Her forward progress halted as if she'd stepped in cement. Her uncle once said instincts acted like ineffective security guards who yelled instructions but couldn't do the thing they advised—that depended on the person doing the actual action. Right now, her mental guards were in a tizzy, yelling *hide, go home,* and even screaming *do not go in the building.* None of them mentioned holding her head up high and entering the building as if all was well, but that's what she had to do. Maybe others trembled around Rita, but she would not be one of them. A peek at Dallas revealed he'd neither seen his ex-wife nor cared where she was.

They reached the open side door and spied people crowding around the display of mouth-watering goodies. Too bad she never got around to whipping up a peanut-butter themed entry.

"Hey, Dallas!" a woman shouted. People turned as a unit in search of the shouter, but at that instant, Tenny spotted a penny on the ground. Her aunt used to say pick up a penny and have good luck all day long. It must be a sign from her aunt as she reached for the heads-up coin. A splat sounded and chunks of meringue and lemon splattered across the floor.

She straightened in time to see Rita with a hand up to her mouth, and then she shot through the crowd. A red-faced woman put both hands on her hips and glared in the direction she took. "They hadn't even judged the pies yet. I just know mine was a winner."

Dallas wiped off a smear of lemony pie filling from his face and popped it into his mouth. "It's a winner in my book. But I'd prefer not to taste it all at once."

The crowd laughed and someone handed him a hand towel, which he used to wipe off most of the pie. He excused himself to the restroom about the time murmurs about Rita started to circulate. Obviously, the pie was meant for her, but Dallas took the brunt when she ducked. A close examination of her outfit revealed a single spot on her skirt. Even beyond the grave, her aunt kept looking after her. The thought calmed her enough to congratulate the winner.

In the future, she'd do a better job of listening to her mental security guards. To be fair, they could have mentioned the pie. Who would have suspected Rita possessed an excellent throwing arm and good aim?

Chapter Twenty-Three

T WILIGHT FELL OVER the fairgrounds. The festive lights strung over the midway glowed enticingly, luring the fair-goers closer. The Ferris wheel ceased its rotation, allowing both Dallas and Tenny to exit with cheerful expressions. Even though the lemon meringue aroma still clung to Dallas, he remained in high spirits. Tenny placed a hand over her heart, uncertain if it could expand any more with all the joy within it. "What an amazing ride! It made the town look like a tiny diorama from the top. I can't remember the last time I've been on the Ferris wheel."

He chuckled and casually reached for her hand. "You and dioramas. Maybe that's where you should put your time instead of a bookmobile."

She smirked. "I considered it once. Not a full-time job, but more of a side hustle. Surprisingly, people do buy dioramas, but they have to be pertinent, such as tied into a historical event, movie, or television show. Fans will drop a hundred dollars or more for a five-inch by eight-inch scene."

"Sounds decent."

"Ha! That's what people would say who don't work in miniatures." They zigzagged their way through the rides, attracting interested glances as they did so. "Buying little tiny books, furniture, or figurines can be pricey. Most enthusiasts create their own, which I do, but that takes time. So, you invest time and money with the hope someone might love it enough to buy it. Otherwise, you're dedicating entire rooms to your collection." She gave his hand a squeeze. "Still, it has merit, especially if I could tie it into something like the town's bicentennial."

"There you go." They neared an alley of game booths. One carnie pointed at Dallas and announced in an overloud, chummy tone, "Surely you're not leaving the place without winning something nice for your gal!"

Rather than dispute the fact that Tenny wasn't his gal, Dallas grinned. "I can give it a go."

Wooden milk bottles were stacked in a pyramid formation. Winning depended on knocking down all the bottles, which often was surprisingly difficult. Often the bottles were hollowed out, then an inserted metal rod made them heavier and less prone to topple. After paying the man, Dallas eyed the bottles and backed up, making sure he was at a right angle to the target before launching a fastball at the bottom row, exploding the formation. The booth guy stumbled back, throwing up his hands either as protection or protest. "I see I got a ringer!"

"Not hardly," Dallas replied. "I spent a lot of time pitching, hoping I'd be the next Roger Clemens."

"You're close," the carnie assured. "Since I know you'll knock all the bottles down and I'd prefer not to be hit by a flying one, go ahead and pick out your prize."

"Tenny?" Dallas asked.

"Dragon." Tenny pointed to a fluffy red and purple dragon. It was smaller than the oversized teddy bears.

"Good choice," the carnie assured.

The three of them—Dallas, Tenny, and the dragon—headed toward the food vendors. As great as the evening had been, with the exception of Rita-related appearances, Tenny longed for fewer crowds, less noise, and definitely less rubbernecking. "Can we get our food and eat back at the house? We can sit in the back yard. I'm sure we'll still be able to hear the fair. It will almost be like being there."

"You don't have to convince me. Let's get our food and go."

Ten minutes later, loaded down with a gyro, a cup of Mexican street corn, pretzel bites, nachos, and a corn dog, they strolled home, greeting people as they did so. An older couple waved at them as they were walking past parked cars, causing them to slow. Dallas introduced them as Mr. and Mrs. McIntyre, his neighbors.

Tenny employed the usual pleasantries, wondering if she should know them. Mrs. McIntyre cleared up the matter.

"George and I are newbies. We've only lived here three years." She gave a little head bob and sniffed. "Long enough to see how disgracefully Dallas' evil ex treated him—and she still causes a ruckus. I'm so glad Dallas has found someone nice and not afraid of…" She shuddered and then spat the words, "…that woman!"

Her husband chuckled. "You'd think she'd been married to your ex as irate as she gets about it."

"It's not right," Mrs. McIntyre insisted. Her husband wrapped an arm around her shoulders and guided her to their car, mumbling their goodbyes.

"You certainly have your champions," Tenny pointed out as they stepped on the sidewalk leading up to her house.

He snorted. "All I have to do is be decent—which is head and shoulders above how Rita acts—and people suddenly think I'm a prince."

They skirted the house until they reached the back yard. The solar fairy lights Tenny had twined around the trees to make backyard time more special glowed, giving the plants and tree silhouettes a mysterious quality. As they settled into some lawn chairs, Tenny broke one of the first rules of dating by bringing up the ex. Since Mrs. McIntyre did it originally, maybe it didn't count. "Guess who I saw up in Beechnut?"

Dallas leaned back in his chair and laced his fingers behind his head. "That would be hard. Since there are so few stores in town, almost everyone goes to Beechnut during the week."

Not as easy as she thought it would be. "How about your least favorite person?"

"Rita." He grimaced, dropped his arms, and reached for his sandwich, unwrapping it as he spoke. "You know how to ruin an appetite. I'm really not surprised."

"Oh?" Her brows arched. "Whatever happened to she only went to the best salons. I didn't think she'd lower herself to plain old Beechnut. Only the best would do for her."

His mouth full, Dallas held up one finger as he swallowed. "That's what she wants people to think. Currently, Mommy and Daddy are bankrolling her. Rumor around town is some bad investments are hovering over their heads like buzzards."

"That explains a lot." Scrambling to her feet, Tenny announced, "I'm going to get us some drinks from the kitchen. I thought seeing Rita and Rand coming out of the seafood restaurant together was a big deal, but apparently not."

"Randall?" He froze in the middle of lifting the gyro to his mouth. "Nerdy, skinny, coke-bottle glasses wearing guy?"

"Obviously, you haven't taken a good long look at him in a while. He no longer wears glasses. From what I saw, he's filled out quite nicely. He goes by Rand now. Don't forget, he now operates the biggest dairy farm around here. Hold that thought while I get us some drinks." Wanting to know Dallas' take on the unusual pairing, Tenny dashed into the house, lunging through the sunroom and grabbing two cold bottles of tea before heading back.

The two glass bottles thumped lightly as she placed them on the table. "Give me your opinion."

"My opinion isn't necessarily the truth. In the short time you were gone, I realized Randall had a huge crush on Rita in high school."

"Who didn't?"

"Me." Dallas pointed to himself. "I messed up big time later, though."

Before she could ask what happened, Dallas placed a finger to his lips. "Now isn't the time. This is our first date and I prefer not to look too much like a fool. You've already witnessed me wearing lemon pie filling—why make it worse?"

Her hand touched his arm. "You were my hero. She intended the pie for me."

"Maybe, maybe not. I can't remember if Rita had a decent aim. I do recall Randall following Rita around with his heart in his eyes. She ignored him, mostly. The thing is, I think he'd do about anything for her. He probably imagines himself as a knight in armor."

"*Anything*, huh?" It opened all sorts of scenarios. "Nothing strange going on at your place?"

"Nope." He crinkled his nose. "Besides, I always thought Randall liked me."

"All's fair in love and war," Tenny interjected but couldn't finger anything that could be laid at Rand's feet. "You know, it could have been just a date. It looked to be a tender goodbye on his part as he crawled into his behemoth of a truck."

"Probably." Dallas remained quiet for a few moments and then asked, "You said he had a big truck?"

"Huge."

"Hmm," Dallas murmured to himself. "You know, he could afford Water Master tires."

As a fan of mysteries, Tenny knew someone being capable of a crime wasn't enough. A lot more people would be behind bars—even if they were innocent. Motivation mattered, along with evidence. Motivation remained murky unless he had intentions of ruining Moo Town, which would be downright rotten. It also made no sense. The next best thing would be evidence. She needed to call Blue right now!

"Ah, look at the time." She pretended to look at her watch, realizing she forgot to put hers on. "You'll need your sleep. The sunflower business never sleeps."

"Tenny…" Dallas paused. "Did I say something wrong? Do something? Are you finally reacting to dating someone who comes with a vindictive ex?"

"No, no. Maybe." She jumped to her feet and paced. "Did you see Rand at the fair?"

"Can't say I did. That doesn't mean he wasn't there." He pointed to the food on the table between them. "You haven't even touched your corn dog or cup of sweet corn."

What a sweetheart, which was unfortunate at this moment. He wouldn't stomp off, and he'd probably discourage her from snooping around Rand's dairy. All the same, it might be the best time while his workers enjoyed the fair.

A familiar chittering occurred, followed by Dallas yelling, "Stop!" He lunged after Precious, who scrambled up a tree with his purloined entrée. "Your critter just took your corn dog!"

Tenny picked up the small cup of street corn and shoveled it into her mouth, barely chewing before swallowing and choking as a result.

Dallas patted her back. "Slow down."

After she ate all but a few kernels, she put the cup down. "Food's gone."

"That it is." He gathered up the debris and placed it in the trash can by the garage, securing the lid. After doing so, he walked up to Tenny and took her hands. "I had a wonderful time. The best I could remember. Now, I don't know what changed things, but can I hope we can try this again? Maybe in a restaurant where you don't have to worry about any wildlife stealing your main course?"

"I'd love to."

Dallas dipped his head, brushing his lips against her forehead before turning and walking away. Even though she desperately needed to share her information with Blue, a couple more seconds watching Dallas couldn't hurt.

Chapter Twenty-Four

SECURITY LIGHTS ATTACHED to each massive barn lit up the darkness, illuminating the central drive and the start of the barbed wire fencing. Late blooming honeysuckle and a reminder of a charcoal barbecue perfumed the air. Blue and Tenny huddled in the shadows near the edge of a field, dressed all in black. For Tenny, this took some doing, but she had snagged a plain black shirt from her aunt's closet, which hung on her slender frame. A locked metal box sat on the floor of her aunt's closet—not one she remembered, which begged investigation if she survived tonight.

"Still a lot of light. I didn't expect when I mentioned Rita and Rand being together and his having a huge truck that we'd be dressed in black, creeping around Rand's farm."

Blue snorted. "You suspected it because you're the one who mentioned that most of his workers would head to the fair."

Fair point. Maybe she *had* thought as much—but thinking about doing something varied a great deal from actually doing it. She chafed her arms even though the temperatures remained warm. Cold sweat trickled down her neck chilling her. "What was our plan again?"

Blue huffed, perhaps irritated that Tenny kept forgetting the plan or, more likely, doubting it. She lowered her voice and edged closer. "We're going to make sure Rupert isn't inside. If he is, I'll snap some photos and we'll call the authorities. We'll have evidence."

As plans went, it lacked a great deal. "What if someone sees us?"

Blue lifted her chin. "We'll say we're on a walk."

"At night?"

"It's cooler."

Tenny gestured to their clothing. "Why are we dressed in black?"

"Obviously, for me," Blue placed one hand on her hip, "it's a slimming option. As for you, an unfortunate choice. Maybe you're embracing your inner Goth."

"Totally believable." Her scrunched expression said the opposite. "The sooner we get this done, the better. You do realize it will take a long time to get law enforcement down here, just in case we find Rupert. Plenty of time for him to be moved again."

Blue stomped her foot. "Darn it! Why do things have to be so hard on the honest people just trying to make a living?"

"People have been asking that question for eons. From now until we get to the car, no talking." Tenny threw up a finger and spoke, breaking her own rule. "What if the barns are locked?"

A dog barked in the distance, and another one answered. "Oh great. They have guard dogs."

"City girl," Blue teased. "Those were coyotes. A dog bit young Rand, which turned him anti-dog. Some say he had it coming. Pulled the dog's ears or tail. It's hard to imagine his having a dog, but I'm not saying he doesn't. We should have brought some dog treats or meat or something."

"Something," Tenny echoed her friend, but before she could point out that her friend failed to answer her question, she spoke.

"On a night like tonight, they'll have all the barn windows open to create a cross breeze. All we have to do is boost ourselves into a stall and then we can have a look around."

"A stall with a two-thousand-pound animal in it."

"Goodness, no." Blue gave an emphatic head shake. "Only bulls weigh that much and because he milks his cows three times a day, I doubt any weigh over a thousand."

"That's reassuring. I assume you'll be the one scrambling into the stall since you're on good terms with cows and all."

Blue squeezed Tenny's arm. "No worries. I'll handle the cows. You can be the security detail."

Ah yes, exactly what a life of reading and research had prepared her for, which translated into she'd be the first one to get bitten by a guard dog if it existed or shot by a trigger-happy employee. "Alrighty." She inhaled deeply. "Let's go."

"One more thing." Blue hugged Tenny, murmuring, "Thanks for being a real friend. The missing Rupert is not only hurting business, but Griffin has sunk into a funk, too. He keeps pointing out all the things that have gone wrong. The litany ends with his saying I'd be better off with someone else."

"We're going to find that bull." Tenny almost added *alive,* but that would draw in the possibility of finding him dead—not something she wanted Blue contemplating. The two of them ended their conversation and kept near the fence.

A flurry of activity near one barn sent them both diving for the grass to flatten themselves the best they could as a pickup truck tore down the drive, spitting gravel onto the pair. For several minutes, they listened while retaining their prone positions. When no voices sounded the alarm, they pushed to their feet, turning slowly and giving the area a full survey. Nothing—except for empty fields and the occasional *moo*.

Blue tiptoed a few steps ahead and motioned for Tenny to do likewise. At first, every moo and every rustle froze them in their tracks, resulting in Tenny's heart racing and her breath held. It took much longer to reach the barns than they originally assumed. Adrenaline rushes faded and their reactions went from frozen in place to a mild study of the area.

At the first barn, not only were the windows propped open, but a few cows had stuck their heads out and *mooed* loudly, as if welcoming them, too. Blue grimaced, placing a finger to her lips as if the cows understood. She peeked in the stalls with Tenny shadowing her. When she finally found one to her liking, she pantomimed the need for a boost by joining her hands together and holding them low, as if to allow someone to step into them. Recognizing the gesture, Tenny knitted her hands together and became a human stepladder that allowed Blue to scramble into the dark stall.

A thump sounded and Blue's arm appeared in the opening, motioning her in. Height served as an advantage, but Tenny had never tried to scramble into a stall before. She placed both hands on the open window and swung her legs upward. The toe of one shoe caught on the edge, and Blue grabbed her leg and pulled her the rest of the way inside. They tumbled into a sprawl of arms and legs onto questionable straw.

The outside lights and moon provided illumination, showing the stall thankfully empty except for two would-be bull rescuers. Even though they'd brought practically nothing with them besides their cell phones, they did have flashlights. Blue guided her out of the stall and into the interior aisle of the barn.

"Light should be less noticeable here," Tenny whispered, flicking on her flashlight and drawing the interest of several cows who responded loudly.

Blue grimaced. "We'll have to work quickly," she hissed. "There's a good chance someone might investigate if the cows start making a ruckus. Sure, cows moo all night, but there's a different tone to the mooing—social mooing as opposed to predator mooing."

"They think we're predators?"

"No. They think it's feeding time. Probably wondering where the night went. Let me try something." She inserted two fingers into her mouth and whistled, a shrill, ear-piercing sound.

A distant, enthusiastic bovine *bellow* answered it.

"Did you hear that?" Blue asked, grabbing Tenny's shoulder in the process.

"The incredibly loud whistle? Yeah, I heard it and so did the surrounding counties."

"No, not that. The answering bellow. It's Rupert! He's here! Not in this barn, though. Let's go!"

Since using the door as an exit didn't serve as an option, Tenny ended up pitching herself out the stall window, curling into a ball to prevent any head injuries. Who knew learning tumbling when she was younger actually came in handy? They sprinted to the second barn, repeating the procedure and riling up the cows, but no Rupert. By the third barn, they found Rascally Rupert cross-tied as if ready to be groomed.

"Jeez." Blue reached to untie the bull while Tenny held the flashlights. Her friend continued a muttered grumbling, probably best left unheard. The bull lowed and rubbed his large head against the compact female.

"All right." Tenny glanced toward the open window where brightness grew along with the rumble of truck engines. "I hate to break up this reunion, but someone's coming—and they're not alone. We need to figure out what to do."

Blue's fingers gripped Rupert's halter. "I can't leave him."

Her gaze flickered between the open window and the growing noise and her friend. Thanks to her uncle Mark, when in a hot spot, Tenny *usually* tried to think logically. "Realistically, it might be hard sneaking him past anyone. Not to mention we forgot to bring a trailer."

"Yeah, about that. I refused to believe Rand would do such a thing. After all, the guy kind of liked me, or at least that was the impression I had."

"Yeah, me, too." Tenny laid the flashlight on the ground and pulled out her phone. She pecked as fast as she could, relating the details to someone who might care.

"What are you doing?" Blue stepped closer while keeping a tight grip on Rupert, which meant he moved closer, too.

"I'm leaving information where we are and what we're doing— just in case we're never heard of or seen again."

Blue swallowed hard.

Total pandemonium broke loose outside. Honking horns, flashing lights, and yelling created just the opening they needed. "Go! It's now or never!"

Chapter Twenty-Five

IN THE DARKNESS of the barn, the grassy aroma of alfalfa blended with the heavier note of manure. Tenny froze, hearing the yells and raised voices outside. The light from her flashlight illuminated Blue holding onto Rupert's halter and forming the words *Turn it off!* Masculine voices shouted questions, a few threw out some unflattering labels, and one voice she easily identified since she'd heard it only an hour before. Dallas.

Curiosity pulled her to an open window where unfamiliar men she assumed were employees kept waving their arms and threatening the new arrivals. The stiff posture, puffed-out chests, and wide stances announced a fight brewing—and possibly the perfect time to sneak out a two-thousand-pound bull. Of course, this would only work if Tenny did her part. She had to open all the stalls, herding the sleeping cows out. Blue warned her they didn't have to be in the field. It was better if they weren't, since all that lovely female company might cause Rupert to lose focus.

The escaping cows would run through the barns and out the open doors, which should give all the employees plenty to do. Dairy cows normally weren't the fleetest of foot, but sometimes, you could get a runner.

Feeling her way along, she moved to the previous barn as Blue exited out the door closest to the field. Only this time, Tenny slipped out an actual door as opposed to throwing herself through a stall window. Someone growled, "Rand! Come out and face the music."

She didn't know who said it, but it didn't sound good. Attention stayed on the main house as Tenny dashed for the second barn but found the door locked. *So untrusting.* It would be the stall window again. Tenny boosted herself up on the lip of an open stall and teetered a little bit, but before she could catch her balance, she fell. *Splat.*

A warm breath dusted her face before a *moo* almost deafened her. Not an empty stall—that's for sure. Not even a clean stall, she soon realized. Yuck! She used straw to clean herself the best she could and swore she'd burn the clothes if she arrived safely home.

No time to be squeamish, she reminded herself. She stood, walked in the direction she thought the door would be and slammed into a wall. "Ouch." She paused, taking time to rub her bruised face and grumbled, "What next?"

Not willing to take chances with her head or any other part of her body, Tenny flicked on her flashlight. Things would go a lot faster if she could see. She opened the stall door and moved out into the aisle. Her most recent roommate just stood there, chewing her cud as opposed to making a break for freedom. Tenny entered the stall and gave the reluctant bovine a push. "Be free! Go! Go!"

Blue never mentioned what to do when a cow wouldn't go. Maybe she thought it wouldn't be a problem. Nothing works like mindless herd mentality. The idea that someone else was doing something got thousands to do likewise. A staple of ad campaigns was to be like whoever was popular by wearing the right shoes, driving the best car, or traveling to the happiest place in the world. If she could get one cow to leave, others would follow. After all, they had to get the term *herd mentality* from somewhere.

She sprinted down the aisle, throwing open more than a dozen stall doors with no takers. What was wrong with them? She raced back down the aisle, noticing cows stirring in their stalls. Most swung their heads around and a few peeked out of their stalls. It was not the stampede she expected where she'd scamper to a high place for safety. With animals that outweighed her, most of them a thousand pounds, they pretty much got to do what they wanted to do.

The memory of a calf in a bigger box stall caused her to break into a jog. Not *all* the cows outweighed her. She eased into the stall, realizing mama cow wouldn't be happy with her idea. She moved toward the calf, making comforting sounds. "Who's the good calf?"

Its ears flicked back and forth, taking in the words, and then it heaved itself awkwardly up and weaved a bit, getting its balance.

"You're the best baby."

The mama cow, still lying down, shot Tenny a suspicious stare and exhaled heavily as if too tired to bother. Even though her best friend lived and breathed cows, Tenny's expertise measured a little above nil. She reached out a hand and patted the calf's soft coat. "Oh, you're beautiful. It's no wonder your mama wants to keep you close."

The calf leaned into her petting, making it easy to grab the tiny halter on its small head. "Let's go for a walk, sweetie."

A slight tug got the calf walking slowly from the stall. Mama cow mooed her protest, slowing the exit of her child, but not halting it. Outside the stall, Tenny kept moving toward the exterior door. She wanted junior to stay safe.

Mama cow followed slowly and kept voicing her upset about the night time walk. Calves were often taken from their mothers and given to nurse cows so the mother could be milked. It made her wonder if mama or surrogate mama followed. Either way more cows peered out of their stalls and a few even stepped out, creating a very slow parade of reluctant participants rather than the expected thunderous herd that would inspire fear. She pushed the sliding door open with a metallic groan and led the calf out.

Other cows streamed out in a casual manner, rather like ladies at a garden party. No rushing. After all, they weren't animals. Only, they were—animals that were constantly fed and milked, not used to running and kicking up their heels as the Moo Town cows did. No wonder Blue assumed they'd hurry out. Instead, they acted more like sleepers waking from a long, confusing dream.

"Hey, Tenny!"

Her hand loosened her hold on the calf's halter and it moved off in search of its mama. Looks like she'd been caught. Running through the numerous explanations of why she was there, she turned to meet the interested stares of both Dallas and Griffin.

"Where's my wife?" Griffin demanded. His shirt buttons and button holes failed to match up, attesting to the speed at which he'd dressed.

"Ah, I really don't know." It was not the answer he wanted, but she could sweeten it. "She's with Rupert. She knew once she told you where he was, the poor animal would vanish again."

Before she could finish, Griffin climbed the fence, landing lightly beside her.

"Here, take my flashlight." Tenny offered it and he accepted. She pointed toward the county road. "I think Blue and Rupert went that way."

Cows mooing, along with a few wayward ones slipping through the open gate, caused a few shouts. Men waved their arms in an effort to corral the adventurous bovines.

Dallas stood next to the fence, facing Tenny. "Are you all right?"

"Smelly, but okay." She tilted her head up. "How about you? What brings you out here?"

He chuckled. "You think you're pretty smart, but you'd be surprised to know I can put two and two together. The good news is I know the sheriff and I may have mentioned women in peril."

Her nose crinkled. Not the women in peril scene. It made them into old movie stereotypes. "I guess my text was unnecessary. We had it under control in a general sense."

"Knowing you, I'm sure you did." He managed a wide smile. "I'm glad you used your myriad of skills to find the bull. Hopefully, now you can concentrate on *other* things."

The emphasis she heard and stored away. "Whatever could Rand's motivation be?"

Chapter Twenty-Six

TRUCK HEADLAMPS, POLICE flashers, and security lights provided enough illumination to observe the sheriff walk a handcuffed Rand to the waiting vehicle. Both Dallas and Tenny stood close enough to hear the complaints.

"Ah, c'mon, Vern!"

"It's Sheriff to you."

"We know each other. Am I the kind of guy that would steal a valuable bull?"

When they had reached the squad car, the sheriff reached around Rand, opened the door, and put his hand on the man's head. "Inside. Obviously, you *are* the type." He shook his head and added, "Your being in the dairy business and all."

"No bull. No evidence," Rand called from the back seat.

A forlorn bovine bellow sounded as Blue, Griffin, and Rupert came into view. Rupert bellowed again, possibly adding his complaints against Rand.

The sheriff reacted first. "It's always good when the evidence arrives on time. Good thing you insisted on bringing your trailer."

Griffin wrapped an arm around Blue. "Yeah, if she thought Rand had Rupert, then he did." He grimaced and then sighed. "I would have liked her to have shared that information as opposed to finding out from Dallas."

"I wanted to be sure," Blue explained with a shrug. "No reason getting you all worked up for nothing."

Before they could continue their discussion, the sheriff interrupted. "I need to leave and process Rand. Am I right in assuming you'll be pressing charges?"

Blue stiffened up and exclaimed, "You'd better believe it! The three of us have been through mental trauma and anguish."

"Three?" The sheriff cleared his throat. "Are congratulations in order?"

"Oh, no." Griffin chuckled. "She meant Rupert. The cows are all our children, and we'd better get this bull home. Dallas, can you help me load the big fellow? He's never a fan of the trailer."

In the next few minutes, the sheriff left with Rand in tow. The various neighbors who'd helped Griffin retrieve his bull gossiped about Rand's motivation as each left. Farm employees returned the captured cows back to their stalls, leaving Blue and Tenny to conduct their own debrief.

Worried she still carried more than a whiff of manure, Tenny backed up a step. "I'm certainly no expert on Rand, but this seems out of character for him. You know what they say, still waters run deep."

"Yeah," Blue acknowledged, adding, "Of course, they usually say that after a murder or murders have been committed. It would make me happy if, somehow, we could finger Rita." She cocked her head to one side. "What would her motivation be?"

"That's a good point." The adrenaline from Tenny's most recent activities faded, leaving exhaustion in its wake. Her shoulders slumped, resulting in her putting one hand on the fence pole for support. "Do you think I smell like manure?"

"Really? That's all you got?" Blue made an expansive gesture to the farm. "There's plenty of manure here. It's hard to say if *you* particularly smell. Personally, I'm surprised. I always thought this was a big deal operation dairy. It's big all right, but the cows aren't being treated right."

"It's as if they never go outside," Tenny remarked. "Back to Rita. As far as we know, our girl only does things that would benefit her. If she were involved, then Rand was the pawn. What type of game is she playing?"

Blue folded her arms and tapped one foot. "She'd really have to hate us to steal Rupert. Was she ever planning on returning him?"

"Hard to say." Uncle Mark's rational thought process of collecting facts first suffered a little without many facts. "Could be she thought it would be easy to get rid of Rupert, and then she found out otherwise."

The loaded trailer and truck stopped near Blue, and Griffin leaned out the open window. "Can I offer my favorite animal detective a ride?"

Blue held up one finger to her husband. Turning to Tenny, she said, "Got to go. You're probably right on the not thinking part. See you!"

Gravel dust kicked up from the trailer as brake lights faded, giving over to the dark night. It looked like the cows were put to bed and all the neighbors rushed home to share the details. If Tenny hoped to find her car, she'd better hurry, especially since Griffin failed to return her flashlight. She placed one booted foot on the bottom wire, keeping a good grip on the fence pole, and swung her leg over, catching her toe on the bottom wire facing the other direction. After repeating the action with the other leg, she hopped to the ground with a bit of pride.

"Wow, you're a regular cow wrangler the way you scaled that fence," Dallas commented as he walked closer. "You need a ride to your car?"

"Possibly." She crinkled her nose. "I'm not getting in your truck. I even hate getting in my own car, but since that's the only way I have to get home, I will. Fortunately, I have seat covers I can tear off and stuff in the washer."

"Fair," Dallas agreed and stuffed his hands into his back pockets. "Could I walk you to your vehicle?"

"How would you find your way back in the dark?" Even though the suggestion appealed, she didn't want to put Dallas out on a dark road. Cars tore down the county roads at a good pace and with the fair going on, there'd be even more drivers—some clueless and others lost.

"I got a tactical flashlight in the truck. Let me grab it." He jogged to his vehicle and returned in a flash. "Let's go."

The two of them walked in tandem as the bright beam lit the way. There was no reason to shorten her stride for the man by her side. Uncle Mark used to joke she was half legs, which wasn't far from the truth. "I'm glad to have Rupert home."

"Not half as glad as Rupert, I bet." He muttered something else under his breath.

"What was that?" She guessed it was something she wasn't supposed to hear.

"Nothing."

"Uh-huh…" Disbelief colored her reply.

"All right, you're going to drag it from me."

Well, she wouldn't call it that.

"Well?"

"I can't help wondering if Rita is the catalyst for this whole thing. If Griffin needed my help, I'd be there. Maybe if things escalated enough, I'd have no time for a certain red-headed librarian. All she needed was a stooge gullible enough to do the heavy lifting."

"I pride myself on my deductive skills, but there's only one thing wrong with your theory." The Dallas she remembered enjoyed solving conundrums and bragging about it just a wee bit.

He coughed but replied with amusement, "Are you saying my theory isn't valid?"

"No, I didn't say that. For all I know, Daddy Dearest might be booking his darling daughter a flight to a non-extradition country even as we speak. So yes, she could be guilty, but she erred in thinking a missing bull would keep you dateless."

"That she did. After you get a good night's sleep, we could take a little road trip. Who knows? It might be the answer to your current quandary."

Her lips twisted as she considered his invitation. As far as answers, it would depend on what *quandary* he meant.

Chapter Twenty-Seven

THE SMELL OF soap clung to Tenny even in her sleep since she had scrubbed numerous times before declaring herself clean. True to her word, she did trash the clothes used for her bull rescue mission, along with the driver-side seat cover. It was time to buy new seat covers—perhaps a pattern that hid spills and stains better than her previous light-colored ones. When she crawled into her bed the night before, she swore she'd sleep ten hours or more.

The memory of Dallas' promised road trip kept her awake longer than she'd liked. Finally, the fair noises ended and all the patrons who parked on her street went home, leaving only the tree frogs and crickets sharing stories in the dark. A scratch came from her window. Something on the screen or tearing the screen in any horror flick would be the escaped killer from the local prison climbing into her window. Part of her knew she should care, but the rest of her didn't have enough energy to do so. Perhaps the killer would overlook her on his mission to wreak vengeance on a town that had done him wrong.

She punched her pillow and snuggled into it, trying to sleep, but instead thinking about scary movies. Often, the bad guy wasn't a random stranger who popped in to terrorize a sleepy hamlet or summer camp, but rather someone who was either neglected or abused in the past. Could that apply to Rand? Was he acting out of vengeance? If so, why target Griffin or Blue? Griffin, as far as she could remember, was a total Boy Scout, both literally and figuratively. No doubt he cut up with the guys now and then. As for Blue, her naturally bubbly personality seldom dimmed.

The scratching at her window stopped, only to be replaced by knocking. Really? What killer knocks on the window in the middle of the night expecting it to be opened by the victim? Vampire, she could understand. Tenny rolled over on her back and cracked her eyes open the tiniest slit, just in case a vile creature of the night hung over her. Sunlight? She squeezed her eyes closed and then slowly opened them. Must not be a vampire. The knocking continued as she pushed up, and it was most definitely her window. Surely her bestie hadn't resorted to practical jokes.

She staggered to the window only to face her nemesis, Precious, staring in at her with his intense black eyes. "I guess you're hungry. Okay, step back," she cautioned as she pushed the window wide to let the raccoon scramble through the shambles of the screen. "However, let's not make a habit of knocking on my window or using it as an entry."

The two made their way to the kitchen where Tenny scrambled eggs for breakfast. After cleaning up, Tenny got dressed, certain someone would appear on her doorstep with details of last night's incident. She didn't have long to wait. When she stepped outside to refill the bird feeders, her neighbor waved her over.

"Did you hear?" The middle-aged woman sporting a bowl haircut and wearing a Minnie Mouse nightshirt started speaking before Tenny even reached the fence.

"Hear what?" Tenny willingly played ignorant, as she didn't

know her role in the re-telling or if she even figured into it at all.

"They found Rascally Rupert the bull up at that big commercial dairy. No surprise. Those big companies are always trying to end the ma and pa businesses." She crossed her arms and bobbed her head.

"Isn't that dairy owned by a local?" There was no reason to say *everything* she knew.

In response, her neighbor walked to her own back door and yelled inside the house. "Hey! Who owns that dairy that did the cow-napping?" She cocked her head and sucked her lips in. "Just as I thought. Okay. Thanks!"

She ambled back over to the fence and announced with a smug expression. "Foreigners own the place."

Foreigners could mean anyone not living in town, from Beech-nut to Sweden. "Alrighty. I'm glad they got their bull back."

Precious chose this moment to exit the house using the dog door. Wait a minute! She eyed the critter who stood up on his hind legs and chittered. If he could use the door, why had he showed up at the window?

Her neighbor was not done talking. "It's not safe anymore. Good thing you have an attack raccoon."

"Oh, it *is* a good thing." Precious' attack abilities centered on food only. "Well, it was nice talking to you." She went back to filling up the feeders and realizing how rumors spread. Halfway through filling the finch feeder with Nyjer seed, she remembered the box and the tiny key on the keyring.

She slipped into her aunt's room, halting for a second to appreciate the lingering fragrance of her Charlie perfume and the memory of Cinnamon singing the Charlie slogan: *A different fragrance that thinks your way.* As the years passed, it became harder and harder for her to find her trademark fragrance, so Uncle Mark bought her a case at a drugstore auction. Her uncle tended to be a bit of an auction hound. If Tenny searched, she'd probably find a half-dozen bottles left, but for now, she'd deal with the mysterious box.

The sliding door opened on the closet with a heavy push, revealing the need for realignment. Between two pairs of well-used shoes sat the box in a prominent position, as if deliberately placed there. It would be hard to miss it and she knew good and well it hadn't been there before. Cinnamon must have put it there right in the front, certain that Tenny would eventually open the closet.

An encouraging presence filtered into the room and the fading perfume grew stronger. Tenny glanced over her shoulder and smiled. She could have sworn a transparent version of her aunt from her younger years took a seat on the bed. The image patted the area beside her, just like her aunt had done so many times before. Her imagination could be working overtime, but the image still comforted her.

The locked box measured approximately sixteen by fourteen inches and turned out to be surprisingly heavy. How did her frail aunt ever position it just so in the closet? Many a time she tried to talk about it, but Tenny refused to listen, unwilling to believe her aunt wouldn't beat cancer. With a bit of a struggle, she hefted the heavy box onto the bed. She pulled the set of keys out of her pocket and tried the first small one with no luck. After all this work, it would be a shame if no key worked. Still, Amos, who bought the hardware store from her uncle, also worked as a locksmith, but Tenny gave her head a shake at the thought. The town of Emerson already had enough to gossip about—why give them anything more?

Carefully, she worked the second unknown key into the lock and it clicked, allowing her to release her held breath. As she opened the lid, she noticed the thick walls of the box, which explained the weight inside the box. Inside were labeled manila folders. The Deed one, she pulled out and discovered the house deed—not too surprising—and another one for some place out in Arizona. She reread the name, but it failed to bring up any memories of Mark and Cinnamon talking about land out west.

Another thick folder held warranties on various appliances. Of course, Uncle Mark had stapled the receipt of the item to the warranty, along with date of purchase. Photos packed another folder—images from years ago when her aunt and uncle were about her age, grinning into the camera, their hair tossed about by the desert wind. Another photo showed a younger red-headed woman looking so much like her, it had to be her mother. Beside her stood a curly brown-haired man with a somber expression. Her fingers traced the image. So long ago and so much unknown... She moved onto the next folder, stuffed full of stocks.

Uncle Mark included a spread sheet of what stocks he owned and what their current worth was. Her eyes widened as she read the names of some of the better known stocks such as Apple and Coca Cola. A sticky note with her aunt's familiar scrawl read that the Coca Cola stock Mark inherited from his father and might be worth something. The Apple stock he bought on his own, when the stock went public in 1980. A second note detailed who their stock broker was and the number at which to reach him. Maybe she could afford that bookmobile and the rehabbing she'd have to do to make it usable.

Overwhelmed, she almost missed the last folder. Unlabeled, she opened it to find envelopes with her name across them. Some were flat like cards; others were thick with folded pages. In the corner, she recognized her mother's name, which made her wonder why had she'd never seen any of these. She turned over each envelope, checking to see if they'd been opened. They hadn't. Stranger. A small ripped page from a memo tablet rested inside the folder. It read:

My Dearest Tenny,

I found these letters and cards when I went through Mark's things. Turns out there was a reason behind his need to be the first one to the mail box. We loved you so much and thought of you as ours. Mark feared your mother would show up and whisk you away. Try to forgive us if you can. When I found the letters, I'd already received my cancer diagnosis, and you chose to stop everything and be with me. Call me selfish, but I didn't want our time together to be tainted by the letters. Hopefully, you and your mother can reconnect.

Just remember whatever we did, if misguided, we did out of love. Often things aren't the way they seemed and folks you think you can trust—you can't. We did the best we could. Be careful. There are some folks out there who mean you harm. Trust your instincts. Use Mark's rational thought process. We'll do our best to watch out for you, too.

All my love,
Aunt Cinnamon

Tenny held the letter, the words blurring, as she pondered *some folks out there who mean you harm.* Was it a general statement like it's a hard world and some people will take advantage of you, or did she mean certain individuals? If so, why not name them? It certainly would make it easier to avoid them. Better yet, could she be referring to anyone in Emerson or even Willow, her mother? The box brought with it a lot more questions than answers.

AN HOUR LATER, Dallas showed up in a polished truck, dashed up the porch steps, and beat out a lively *tap-tap* on the door. The door swung open, revealing a smiling Tenny. "I felt sure that it wasn't Precious. I left him in the back yard, which he isn't a fan of, in hopes he'll reconnect with nature."

"Good luck with that. I thought you might like to take a little drive to the next county to my aunt's house."

"You have relatives in the area?" This surprised her since she assumed Dallas' family moved to Emerson because of a church assignment.

"It's my father's sister, which is one of the reasons he took the Emerson church. The other reason is he hoped it would be a slower pace and a peaceful atmosphere."

"What's your take?" Tenny couldn't resist asking after last night.

"Most of the time, it is quiet and leisurely. I guess now and then we need a little something to shake us up so that we appreciate the other times."

"Hmm." She hummed her reply and narrowed her eyes. "Personally, I could do without the shakeup moments. I've had all too many of them recently."

"That's why I'm here. I promised a possible solution to one of your issues, plus a picnic, and the lowdown on Rand, too. My cousin works in the sheriff's office, and she was there when they brought

Rand in."

"Is your cousin the daughter of the aunt we're planning to see?"

"She is. My aunt often watches her little girl for her. We might meet all three if we hurry."

Dallas acted as if it would be a good thing to meet three of his relatives in one fell swoop. It felt more like an opening for a reality show with the announcer saying, "What could go wrong?!" Then the canned laughter would sound.

"Okay. Let me grab my bag and lock up. My neighbor tells me it's not safe around here with foreigners trying to ruin local businesses. Good thing I have a guard raccoon."

"Ha!" Dallas snorted. "You need a guard to watch out for Precious." He waited until she locked the door and cupped her elbow as they walked down the front steps.

Certain her neighbor watched, ready to spread the news of her dating life, Tenny waved as they drove away. She felt happy and rather pleased to be the center of gossip, but in a good way, as opposed to being that poor, motherless girl. The road widened as they left town, and the speed limit increased. There were no more smiles and nods at folks they knew, or Dallas knew. Now, she could get the details. "Spill. I've waited long enough."

"Wouldn't you want to hear it from my cousin?" Dallas teased.

Sure, she'd want to wait however long it would take to arrive and listen to the reason behind the conflict that hung over her and her friends' lives like a dark cloud the entire week. "Nope. You're lucky I've waited this long."

Tenny reached around the wooden picnic basket and nudged him. "Come on."

"It's a long and twisted tale," he warned.

"Quit stalling." She placed one hand on the door handle. "I might have to get out and walk if you don't stop teasing me."

"Don't do that." He slowed and shot her a concerned look. "Apparently, by the time Rand arrived at the sheriff's office, he was over his it's-all-a-mistake whining. Instead, he blamed everything on…" Dallas paused. "Do you want to guess?"

"Rita?" She clapped her hands together, hoping the Queen of Mean would get her comeuppance.

"No, Blue."

"Blue?" Her mouth fell open. "How can that be? She certainly didn't steal her own bull."

"He said he always wanted to be worthy of Blue. That's why he went into the dairy business. Griffin worked with cows. *He* decided to do likewise. All the things he did to make Blue fall for him didn't work. That's when he started his campaign against Moo Town. Little things at first."

Tenny touched Dallas' arm, stopping the discussion. "Did he really say all this? I know in books and movies you have the bad guy confessing all, but who does that? It makes no sense."

"Cindy wouldn't lie. Besides, I think Rand feels like it's a defense. *I was so in love with Blue that I couldn't help myself.* Plenty of men have used this defense for harassing, kidnapping, or even killing the object of their love."

"I hope none of them went free. What about my seeing Rand with Rita at the seafood place? That's not the behavior of a man so in love with Blue."

"Yeah, that. You'll like this." He smirked. "Shamefully, I like it *too* much. Turns out Rita thought they were on a date. Rand felt as if people were giving him the eye like they *knew*. Most everyone knew about his crush on Blue. He thought it wise to be seen with someone else. Who better than Emerson's unofficial queen?"

"Oh." Her mouth took the shape of the word. "If she finds out, it will kill her to discover she was the pawn for a change."

Dallas hooted with laughter. "Sorry. I know I'm being petty, but it's unusual for the shoe to be on the other foot when it comes to Rita. Ok, we're almost to my aunt's place."

That brought up the reason for the trip. Hopefully, she wasn't meeting the only local relatives to get their approval before seeing Dallas. After Rita, she'd understand why they might want to be involved. "We're visiting your aunt why?"

He turned on his blinker and veered onto a gravel road. "It's my uncle's old camper. *Van* might be a better description. He was always coming up with inventions and ideas. He converted a small camper into a Movies and Dinner Delivery service. This was way before all the food delivery apps, and movies were on VHS tapes. He'd pick up the food folks ordered, keep it warm in a thermos box, and when he arrived, the family could look through the movies in his collection by stepping into the van. He also sold candy and ice cream."

"No popcorn?"

Dallas slowed as he passed a series of dwarf apple trees and turned by a sign shaped like an apple emblazoned with *Help Yourself! You-Pick-It Orchard.* "We're here. As for popcorn, he might have sold some microwave bags. As you know, VHS went out, as did people renting movies, and the camper has been sitting in the barn since then. It's in fair shape but will need new tires and a tune-up. It already has shelves for VHS tapes that should fit books."

A barking border collie kept pace with the truck as two women exited the brick house. The older one had a checked apron over her clothes, while the younger one, attired in jeans and a T-shirt, waved.

Dallas stopped the truck and turned to Tenny. "How do you want me to introduce you? I could introduce you as my friend, visiting librarian, or sleuth extraordinaire?"

Uncle Mark, who loved his quotes, would say *start as you mean to finish*. She inhaled deeply, smiled, and said, "Tell them I'm the Bookmobile Gal."

Epilogue

SATURDAYS WERE RATED as one of the busiest days for the carwash. Water squirted and pooled in the various bays while car washers blasted music from their vehicles or hooted as they tried to spray one another—mainly the younger ones.

The sun shone down on the freshly washed Book Van. Blue insisted the best color for the bus should be blue, insisting it would be relaxing. A soft green served as Tenny's choice. It reminded her of reading outdoors under the leafy maple tree. Because it was her van, she went with an outdoor mural of kids, dogs, and adults lounging on the green grass under a blue sky with a book in hand and a stack of books beside them. In bold letters on all four sides, it read: The Book Mobile. Smaller cursive script underneath The Book Mobile stated *Your Adventure Begins Here.*

"Looks good." Tenny placed her hands in her back pockets as she admired her latest acquisition. Much had changed in the last six weeks, and mainly her attitude. She went from *what* in the world was she going to do next in her life to knowing what she *would* do and being excited about the fact. She'd emailed her former boss and told her thanks for the offer, but an exciting opportunity to be her own boss superseded it.

"Much better than when it was dinner and a movie on wheels. It sounded too much like a person wolfing down a burger while driving and trying to watch a movie at the same time." Dallas grinned, throwing out one hand in the van's direction. "If the van even looked half as good as this, my uncle would have gotten more looks, and in turn, more business." He pointed to the spot under the lettering. "What you need right there is a website or social media address."

"Website? Social media address?" Tenny's voice squeaked. Had she really thought it would be quite enough to paint a vehicle and stick books inside? She'd even worked out a tentative schedule with the surrounding townships and a few primary schools with no libraries. "Do I really need that?"

"Depends." Her blond beau and occasional bookmobile helper placed one hand on his hip. "If you want to reach more people, especially those who use social media, you do. You'd be surprised who uses social media, too. My granny has her own website. Mainly she posts family photos and recipes, but she's still online."

He had a point, and a valid one, too. "Ah, I'm not the techiest person. I list books on the online catalog, order stuff online, and send out emails. The social media stuff baffles me."

Blue laughed, but Tenny continued, "I might need help with setting up the website and whatever. So, why do I need this?"

"Think of it as free advertising." Dallas smirked, but continued, "When people want to know when the bookmobile is in their area, they go online. You can add a calendar. I have a cousin who does website design, and you already met her when we looked at the van."

"Oh! Oh!" Blue interjected and waved an upraised hand as if in class. "Just think! You can announce events, such as book clubs, special drawings, or photos with Santa."

"Photos with Santa," she echoed Blue's words. "Wow! This thing is snowballing. I can see merit in creating special reading themes, though. Maybe we can have book drives where people donate new and used books and we give them away to those who want them."

A couple of teenagers washing their vehicles wandered over to where the trio stood.

The dark-haired girl wearing a Japanese anime shirt pointed to the van. "Is that going to be around here?"

"Yes, it will," Blue answered before Tenny could. "Are you interested?"

"Will it have manga novels? Graphic novels are my jam." She pointed to her eyes. "Visual."

Tenny pulled out her phone and opened the note app and typed in *manga books* under things to buy. She glanced up and addressed the anime fan. "Can you recommend any popular manga books?"

Her companion nudged her, and she spoke fast as if she'd just been waiting for that exact question. "Popular right now are *The Apothecary Diaries*, *Kingdom*, *Dr. Stone*, *Tokyo Revengers*, and *My Hero Academia*. Make sure they're in English. I've accidentally bought some in Japanese." She shrugged. "I kept it for my collection, though."

Tenny made her repeat the list at a much slower pace. "Got it. I appreciate the list."

Her companion, a wiry male, cleared his throat. "Will you have any do-it-yourself books?"

"Like what?" Tenny inquired, opening her note app again.

"For fixing engines, both regular and diesel. I'm a mechanic, or at least trying to be one."

"Sounds like a great idea!" Tenny added the suggestion to her list.

The couple thanked her, but before walking away they asked, "When is the bookmobile thing happening?"

Tenny stalled with the word, *soon.*

Blue covered her awkwardness. "We'll keep you informed on the website."

Helpful, but not helpful, because she knew they would ask.

Almost on cue, the girl said, "What's the website?"

Blue, ever inventive, pursed her lips as if to speak, but Dallas beat her to it. "Tenny's Book Adventures Bus dot com. No apostrophe in the web address. It's not up yet, but it will be."

The couple thanked him, waved, and returned to washing their vehicle.

"Where did this name come from? Did you just pull it out of the air?" Tenny narrowed her eyes at the man deciding her bookmobile name.

"Not exactly. I took The Book Mobile and your slogan and had my cousin check on various existing websites last night. As you can guess, The Bookmobile and variations of it have been taken, along with reading adventures. She kept trying until she found a free domain by rearranging pertinent words, which we reserved for you. But…" He lengthened the last word and gave her the sad puppy dog eyes. "…if you don't like it, feel free to make up your own."

"Tenny's Book Adventures Bus. It has a nice ring to it." She wanted to be mad at him, but she knew he was just trying to help— just like Uncle Mark and stowing away the letters. It would be nice to be consulted, especially when it involved her. Inhaling deeply, she considered her words. "The name works for me, but…" She shook her index finger at Dallas. "…don't go deciding anything else about my book bus without informing me."

There was no reason to add that she had enough on her plate with her unopened letters and a vague reference by her aunt Cinnamon to be on guard against certain people—maybe that was the pain medicine. Then again, what if it wasn't? She might as well change the subject. "Blue, whatever happened to your dairy helper, Cody?"

"Ha! Him? He vanished about the time Rand got arrested. Never the best worker, so when he didn't show up the first time, no biggie. He never showed up again after that. Those little problems we kept having, such as things going missing and the milking machines getting messed up, stopped when Cody left, which could be a coincidence or maybe not. Goes to show people can fool you. Griffin felt sorry for him and wanted to help him out. It could have been an act just to lure my hubby into hiring him." She clicked her tongue. "Do you ever really know anyone?"

Good question, but right now, Tenny would concentrate on making the moving library a reality. "Okay, bookmobile squad, let's clean the inside. Apparently, I have a great deal to do today, including hiring someone to create a website and ordering books. Adventures await the bookmobile."

Blue, who sometimes liked to have the last word, snapped open the van's sliding door and winked as she did so. "Wouldn't be surprised if there aren't a few mysteries along the way."

The End

Bullies, Bovines and a Bookmobile Recipes

Easy Cinnamon Rolls

Courtesy of Red Star Yeast

Prep Time: 1 hour, 40 minutes

Cook Time: 25 minutes

Total Time: 2 hours, 5 minutes

Yield: 10-12 rolls

Ingredients

DOUGH
- 2 and ¾ cups (344g) **all-purpose flour**
- ¼ cup (50g) **granulated sugar**
- ½ teaspoon **salt**
- ¾ cup (180ml) **whole milk**
- 3 Tablespoons (45g) **unsalted butter**
- 2 and ¼ teaspoons **Platinum Yeast from Red Star** or any instant yeast *(1 standard packet)*
- 1 large **egg**, at room temperature

FILLING
- 3 Tablespoons (45g) **unsalted butter**, extra softened
- 1/3 cup (67g) packed light or dark **brown sugar**
- 1 Tablespoon **ground cinnamon**

CREAM CHEESE ICING

- 4 ounces (113g) full-fat block **cream cheese**, softened to room temperature
- 2 Tablespoons (30g) **butter**, softened to room temperature
- 2/3 cup (80g) **confectioners' sugar**
- 1 teaspoon **pure vanilla extract**

Instructions

1. **Make the dough:** Whisk the flour, sugar, and salt together in a large bowl. Set aside.
2. Combine the milk and butter in a heatproof bowl. Microwave or use the stove and heat until the butter has melted and the mixture is warm to the touch (about 110°F/43°C, no higher). Whisk in the yeast until it has dissolved. Pour mixture into the dry ingredients, add the egg, and stir with a sturdy rubber spatula or wooden spoon OR use a stand mixer with a paddle attachment on medium speed. Mix until a soft dough forms.
3. Transfer dough to a lightly floured surface. Using floured hands, knead the dough for 3 minutes. You should have a smooth ball of dough. If the dough is super soft or sticky, you can add a little more flour. Place in a lightly greased bowl (I use non-stick spray), cover loosely and let the dough rest for about 10 minutes as you get the filling ingredients ready.
4. **Fill the rolls:** After 10 minutes, roll the dough out in a 14×8-inch (36×20-cm) rectangle. Spread the softened butter on top. Mix the cinnamon and brown sugar. Sprinkle it all over the dough. Roll up the dough to make a 14-inch log. Cut into 10–12 even rolls and arrange in a lightly greased 9- or 10-inch round cake pan, pie dish, or square baking pan.
5. **Rise:** Cover the pan with aluminum foil, plastic wrap, or a clean kitchen towel. Allow the rolls to rise in a relatively warm environment for 60–90 minutes or until double in size.
6. **Bake the rolls:** After the rolls have doubled in size, preheat the oven to 375°F (190°C). Bake for 24–27 minutes, or until lightly

browned. If you notice the tops are getting too brown too quickly, loosely tent the pan with aluminum foil and continue baking. If you want to be precise about their doneness, their internal temperature taken with an instant-read thermometer should be around 195–200°F (91–93°C) when done. Remove the pan from the oven and place it on a wire rack as you make the icing. (You can also make the icing as the rolls bake.)

7. **Make the icing:** In a medium bowl using a handheld or stand mixer fitted with a paddle or whisk attachment, beat the cream cheese on high speed until smooth and creamy. Add the butter and beat until smooth and combined, then beat in the confectioners' sugar and vanilla until combined. Using a knife or icing spatula, spread the icing over the warm rolls and serve immediately.

8. Cover leftover frosted or unfrosted rolls tightly and store them at room temperature for up to 2 days or in the refrigerator for up to 5 days.

Notes

1. **Make-Ahead Instructions:** This dough can be made the night before through step 4. Cover with plastic wrap and let rest in the refrigerator overnight. The next morning, remove from the refrigerator and allow to rise in a warm environment for about 1 hour. Continue with step 6.

2. **Freezing Instructions:** Baked rolls can be frozen for up to 2–3 months. Thaw overnight in the refrigerator and warm up before enjoying. You can also freeze the unbaked rolls and here's how: bake the rolls in step 6 for only about 10 minutes at **375°F (190°C)**. Cool completely, then cover tightly and freeze. To serve, take the pan of rolls out of the freezer and put it into the refrigerator a few hours before serving. Then, finish baking them for the remaining 15–18 minutes.

3. **Yeast:** I highly recommend instant yeast. If you only have active dry yeast, you can use that instead. Active dry and instant yeast

can be used interchangeably in recipes (1:1). Active dry yeast has a moderate rate of rising and instant dry yeast has a faster rate of rising; active dry yeast will take longer to raise the dough.

4. **Milk:** This recipe used to call for ½ cup (120ml) milk and ¼ cup (60ml) water. The rolls taste much richer using all milk, and that is what I recommend. Whole milk or even buttermilk are ideal for this dough. If needed, you can substitute ¾ cup (180ml) lower-fat or nondairy milk.

5. **Coffee Icing (or Vanilla Icing):** Whisk 1 cup (120g) of confectioners' sugar, ½ teaspoon pure vanilla extract, and 2–3 Tablespoons (30–45ml) strong brewed coffee together until smooth. Or swap milk for coffee for regular vanilla icing. Drizzle over warm rolls.

Peanut Butter Streusel Coffee Cake

From "**Stay for Supper**" by the Editors of *Country Home* magazine (1993).

This is not a coffee cake where you can make the batter and make the streusel at the same time.

Equipment

- 1 8 x 8 x 2 pan
- Stand Mixer

Ingredients

Peanut Butter Streusel Topping
- ¼ Cup Flour
- ¼ Cup Light Brown Sugar Packed
- 2 Tablespoons Peanut Butter
- 1 Tablespoon Butter
- ¼ Cup Mini Chocolate Chips (I typically use regular-sized chips)

Coffee Cake
- 2 Tablespoons Butter
- ¼ Cup Peanut Butter
- 1 Cup Flour
- ½ Cup Light Brown Sugar Packed
- ½ Cup Milk
- 1 Large Egg
- 1 teaspoon Baking Powder
- ¼ teaspoon Baking Soda
- ¼ teaspoon Salt
- ¼ Cup Mini Chocolate Chips (here, too, I use regular-sized chips usually)

Instructions

1. Heat oven to 375*.
2. Grease an 8 x8 8x 2 pan with Baker's Joy or Pam for Baking with Flour and set aside.
3. Combine the first four topping ingredients with a pastry blender or a spoon in a small bowl.
4. Stir in the ¼ of Chocolate Chips. Set aside.

For the Coffee Cake

Add the Peanut Butter and the Butter to the bowl of an electric stand mixer and combine for 30 seconds.

1. Pour in about half of the 1 Cup of Flour, all the Brown Sugar, half of the Milk, the Egg, Baking Powder, Baking Soda, and the Salt. Mix until combined, scraping the sides of the bowl on occasion.
2. Add in the rest of the Flour and the Milk. Beat until JUST combined and then STOP. Do NOT keep beating this to death.
3. Stir in the Chocolate Chips by hand. It is so easy to go from "not combined" to "mixed within an inch of its life" when you use a stand mixer.
4. Pour the batter into the greased pan and spread it around the best you can. Top with the, uh, topping.
5. Bake 375* for 25-30 minutes or until a toothpick near the center comes out clean.
6. Cool on a wire cooling rack for 15 minutes to set. Serve warm.

Tenny's Peanut Butter Muffins

These peanut butter muffins are delicious.

Prep Time: 15 mins

Cook Time: 15 mins

Total Time: 30 min

Ingredients

- 1 ¼ cups all-purpose flour
- ¾ cup rolled oats
- ¾ cup brown sugar
- 1 tablespoon baking powder
- ½ teaspoon salt
- 1 ¼ cups milk
- ¼ cup peanut butter
- 1 egg

Directions

1. Preheat oven to 375 degrees F (190 degrees C).
2. Mix flour, oats, brown sugar, baking powder, and salt in a large bowl. Beat milk, peanut butter, and eggs in another bowl; stir into oat mixture, mixing until the batter is well blended. Spoon batter evenly into 12 muffin cups.
3. Bake in the preheated oven until a toothpick inserted into the center comes out clean, 15 to 18 minutes.

Frogs, Floods, and Fraud

Available June 2023

THE AUTUMN AFTERNOON sun slipped through the parted gingham curtains warming the late lunch crowd and those who chose to indulge themselves with one of Almost Home Café's delectable desserts. Silverware clattered against sturdy stoneware plates as customers gorged themselves on chicken fried steak, apple dumplings, and local gossip. Even when a person chose not to pass along idle chatter and rumors, it failed to stop ears from hearing. Tenny, Emerson's newest resident and official bookmobile owner, picked up her fork and used it to test the flakiness of her apple dumpling. After her Aunt Cinnamon passed, the thirty-ish former reference librarian found herself comparing every morsel she consumed to the delicious dishes her aunt made. Her aunt's award winning cinnamon rolls earned her aunt her nickname. Cinnamon had even contributed desserts to the café. No other cooks even came close. Although, the crust on the dumpling did flake nicely. She speared a bite, sampled it, swallowed, and sighed. "This is really good. Did they get someone new in the kitchen?"

Blue, Tenny's best friend and current companion, tucked a lock of her chin-length blonde hair behind her ear. "You bet. Otherwise, I wouldn't have suggested dropping in for a treat." She patted a rounded hip. "I can't afford any wasted calories on a tasteless concoction. Heard it was Philomena's grandson. You probably don't remember him. He was about eight years behind us in school, which makes him about twenty-two now."

"Whoever it is, he knows his way around a pastry cutter." Tenny loaded her fork with the glistening apples and feather-light crust. Her nose scrunched up and she lowered her fork to her plate, the delicious forkful uneaten at the first hint of overheard nasty gossip since it contained her first name.

The woman's voice carried, loud enough for everyone in the small diner to hear. "I'm just saying, Dallas only went out with Tenny out of pity, ya know? With her aunt dying and all. Trust me, I have the details."

Blue reached across the table, nudging her friend's arm. "Ignore her. Shadow's only carrying out Rita's bidding. As far as Dallas dating people to cheer them up, you'd be the first." She smirked, then winked.

"Yeah." If anyone should know up close and personal the machinations of the town's self-appointed queen, Tenny should— especially since she stepped out with the queen's ex enough times to cause speculation. While she wanted to chalk it up to malicious gossip, it did make her wonder. *What if Dallas only asked her out of kindness?* "Ah, let's talk about something else."

"Ready to do your first bookmobile run?" Blue asked as she finished up her apple dumpling and gave Tenny's uneaten portion a speculative glance.

Noticing her gaze, Tenny pulled the plate closer. "I intend to finish it, even if I do it at home." She inhaled deeply, then spoke. "As for the first run, technically I'm ready, but..." she sucked in her lips and shook her head, "I'm a little worried. Sure, I know this was my aunt's dream and all. I'm not even all that good at driving an extra-long van, especially on all those narrow, winding country roads."

"Practice." Blue bobbed her chin with a touch of certainty. "We'll take the bookmobile for a dry run of sorts."

Before she could ask for more details, their server swung by with a coffee carafe and topped off their cups. The server, a middle-aged woman sporting gray streaks that resembled Bride of Frankenstein's hairdo, or at least it drew that comparison around Halloween, delivered food and drink with a side of chatter. "Did you hear," she started, "that Rivertown has to move? Turns out flood insurance stops paying out after so many floods. Personally," she propped her free hand on her waist as if settling in for a lengthy conversation, "they should have called the place *Floodsville*." A bark of laughter punctuated her comment. No one else chuckled.

Tenny noted her friend's furrowed brow and pinched lips, then remembered. "Don't you have relatives in Rivertown?"

"Yes." The normally gregarious Blue's one-word answer hinted at much more, better told in another place.

Not deterred by the mono-syllabic comment, the server cleared her throat and added, "You better get the spare room cleaned out because you're probably having company."

Both Blue and Tenny shot each other befuddled looks before turning back to their waitress. "Um," Tenny tried to remember her name, then noticed her neatly printed name tag, "Sally. Are you doing psychic readings along with delivering pie?"

"Ha! Ha!" She barked out the laugh. "I don't remember you being funny, but people change, I suppose." Sally pursed her lips as if she doubted the possibility of Tenny ever coming up with a funny or two.

It didn't seem like that needed a comment, but she did need to know where Sally was going with her conversation. When it came to getting information, Blue usually jumped in feet first, but not today. This morning it would be up to Tenny. "How did you get all this information? Online?"

"Mercy, no. You can't believe what all these kids are putting online. They make up half of that stuff. My cousin's sister married a man from Rivertown. He's got people there." She leaned forward and put up a flattened hand to the side of her mouth as if to shield her from possible lip readers. "Story is, the town council presented their case to both the state and federal government for assistance to moving higher up. They both ponied up some funds. I even heard they started a Go Fund Me account that raised a lot. Anyhow, everything was ready to go, when the money vanished!" She placed the coffee carafe on the table and snapped her fingers. "Like that. It's gone! That's why I said you better plan on company. I imagine your relatives will be headed this way soon."

A town moving should be relatively big news, but a town losing all its money in one fell swoop should be even bigger news. Odd she hadn't heard about it. To be fair, she hadn't been watching the news due to spending all her time fixing up the bookmobile. "How come I haven't heard of this?"

Using three fingers, Sally tapped her own chest. "*I* just found out about it. No worries. As soon as they catch that Tessa Singleton, they'll have their money."

"Tessa?" A paler than usual Blue squeaked out the name.

"Yep!" Sally concurred. "The money vanished about the same time she did. It had to be her."

Someone behind them said loudly, "What does a person have to do to get a cup of coffee around here?"

Sally sniffed and picked up the carafe while muttering, "Some people."

"Okay." Grateful for the interruption, Tenny stood, scooping up her apple dumpling. "I'm going to get a box for this and pay. We're getting out of here. I'll meet you outside."

Her friend wordlessly slid out of the booth and out the front door. Obviously, something was up. Thankfully, they had already rescued Blue and Griffin's prize bull, Rascally Rupert, so it couldn't be that. She read once on a T-shirt that good friends are ones who help you hide the body. Nope. Good friends are the ones who help you turn an aging conversion van into a bookmobile, which required much more work than hiding a body. It was her turn to be the supportive friend. After what felt like twenty minutes, Sally took her money and boxed her dessert while implying Tenny should eat more pie to fill out her skinny frame.

Bolting out the door with her to-go box in hand, she spotted Blue texting on her phone next to a dusty pickup truck. A few long strides brought her abreast with her friend. "What's up?"

Blue glanced up, bit her bottom look, then spoke. "Tessa is my cousin." She inhaled deeply and stomped one foot. "I know for a fact she wouldn't have taken the money. As for vanishing, I'm not surprised. That's been her only goal in life to leave Rivertown. We *have* to find her. She has no clue she's being framed for a crime. What should we do first?"

Sure, her bestie's wide eyes and climbing colors denoted her outrage but Blue stayed loyal to the end. Maybe her cousin helped herself to the funds or maybe she didn't. A good friend would help clear the cousin's name until it became obvious the cousin was as dirty as a pig in a mud puddle. "I say we have our dry run trip. Rivertown, here we come!"

Bullies, Bovines, and A Bookmobile
Author Notes

Readers often ask what's the inspiration for a series. Many authors have grand explanations of how it came to them in a dream or in a flash while riding a train through the French countryside. Others simply write about what is trending and are fast enough to keep up with the ever-changing world of fiction. Then, there's me, I'm more of a write-what-you-know author. When it comes to small towns, cows, and libraries, I come by them naturally.

My childhood consisted of feeding chickens and occasionally tying my sister up to a clothesline post, then riding away on my pinto pony. Small towns have been a big part of my life. I realize every town, burg, or village isn't the same. The fictional place of Emerson is based on a few of the small towns I know. By this time in my life, I've worked in five different libraries, including a university library.

The characters are a combination of characteristics from people I've met and worked with along with some influence from childhood television. No character is directly taken from any work or totally based on one person. As for the cow element, I grew up with a dairy cow we named Elsey. Later on, I went to work at an organic grass-fed dairy. I've even visited dairies the way some people drop by antique shops.

Finally, if you are wondering about Precious, the raccoon, I did have a neighbor who raised a baby raccoon and kept it in the house. Even though the story is fictional, many of the details are real such as the 4-H animal show classes. Tenny's insistence on only entering peanut butter items goes back to my own daughter who refused to do the baking class requirement for the year, such as biscuits or pretzels, and simply made what she wanted with the help of her grandmother. While she didn't win any ribbons for her single-mindedness, the judges did enjoy her creations.

I hope you enjoyed this tale and get ready for the next book in the series, **Frogs, Flood, and Fraud**, which is coming June 2023.

Do you want to know more about the series and upcoming releases? Join the newsletter and get all the book info, personal appearances, and giveaways. Go to www.morgankwyatt.com and sign up. If you liked **Bullies, Bovines, and a Bookmobile**, remember the best way to encourage an author to write more is by leaving a review. ☺

Made in the USA
Middletown, DE
06 January 2023